A Witch Across Time

BOOKS BY GILBERT B. CROSS

A Hanging at Tyburn
Mystery at Loon Lake
Terror Train

A Witch Across Time

GILBERT B. CROSS

Atheneum   1990   New York

Atheneum
Macmillan Publishing Company
866 Third Avenue
New York, New York 10022
Collier Macmillan Canada, Inc.

First Edition
Printed in the United States of America
Designed by Nancy Williams
10 9 8 7 6 5 4 3 2 1

Library of Congress Cataloging-in-Publication Data
Cross, Gilbert B.
    A witch across time/by Gilbert B. Cross.—1st ed.
      p. cm.
    Summary: Spending the summer with her great-aunt on Martha's Vineyard while recovering from a period of emotional imbalance, fifteen-year-old Hannah encounters the ghost of a young woman, who was executed as a witch in 1692 and seeks to clear her name.
    ISBN 0-689-31602-X
    [1. Witchcraft—Fiction. 2. Ghosts—Fiction. 3. Martha's Vineyard (Mass.)—Fiction. 4. Emotional problems—Fiction.]
    I. Title. PZ7.C88252Wi 1990 [Fic]—dc20
89-38474 CIP AC

For
Peggy, John, and Robert,
the Rhinoskins,
and Dori, for the letters

Part I

STATUES IN A DARK HALL

Part II

A WITCH ACROSS TIME

Part 1
Statues in a Dark Hall

1
Islander

HANNAH KINCAID STOOD ALONE BY THE RAIL OF the car ferry, *Islander*, as it moved steadily toward Vineyard Harbor, its huge bathtub shape churning the blue water to a foaming wake. To her right, at the end of the seawall, stood a miniature lighthouse striped red and white like a giant barber pole. Ahead, she could see the town with its church steeple and white-painted saltbox houses, their dark green roofs set among tall elm trees. Atop many houses facing the sea were widow's walks bordered by low iron railings.

A gust of wind played with Hannah's dark brown hair; briefly she thought of combing it, but the idea seemed silly. At least she no longer wore it so long that she constantly had to tuck it behind her ears when she talked. As her friend Melanie put it, "One adjusts, my dear. One adjusts."

She smiled, despite her apprehension. When she had arrived at Reach Out Academy, Melanie Anne Richards had come up to her immediately, peered at her, and said, "It's not a beautiful countenance. Oval faces seldom are, but the brown eyes give you a sort of Bambi look. And a slender nose is nothing to lament, my dear." While Hannah had waited for the ground to swallow her up, Melanie had added, with a smile, "Hi. I'm Melanie, the mother superior of our little home away from home."

That was two years ago; they were thirteen then, and Melanie was already beautiful. She had clear white skin, blue-green eyes under a dark fringe of lashes, and the high cheekbones of a model. Her most arresting feature, however, was a heart-shaped face surrounded by a wild explosion of bright red, naturally curly hair. By the end of a week, the two had become closer than sisters. The gold hoop earrings Hannah now wore were a going-away present from Melanie.

Around her, people were on the move. The *Islander*'s horn sounded, long and mournful. It passed small vessels of every shape and size, many at their moorings. A girl on a jet ski skimmed toward the ferry, and the horn sounded several short, urgent blasts. With a cheery wave, she turned away. A passenger near Hannah muttered contemptuously, "Crazy off-islander."

Hannah had already heard the term and knew it was used to refer to anyone who hadn't been born on Martha's Vineyard. She shrugged. Now she was to become an off-islander.

Reversing engines, the ferry edged carefully toward the Steamship Authority pier. From the rail Hannah had an excellent view of the fishing fleet. Men in soiled T-shirts and peaked caps were gutting fish. The boats all looked alike: a small cabin toward the front and thin planks fastened to the sides of the boat to keep sea and spray out.

As the men cleaned the fish, they tossed the unwanted

pieces overboard. Gulls circling overhead were incredibly quick to dive. One flew just past Hannah's reach; the sun caught the gray extended wings; they flashed briefly as the bird wheeled. An instant later, without seeming to have touched the water, the bird was sweeping aloft, a great piece of raw fish in its curved beak.

The *Islander* neared its mooring; as the sides of the ferry nudged the huge wooden dock, several crewmen threw heavy ropes over the rail. Great rubber tires cushioned the shock, but still there were grinding protests from the wooden pilings.

Hannah looked at her watch. Six-thirty exactly. The ferry was on time. At least her aunt hadn't been forced to wait for her.

A voice over the loudspeaker urged the foot passengers to wait until the vehicles were driven off. No one paid any attention. There was a rush forward. Vacationers poured from every deck and room, loaded with surfboards, sleeping bags, portable radios, and huge rucksacks. Hannah looked around and was soon convinced she was the only person with an ordinary suitcase. But then she was probably the only passenger who wasn't arriving for a vacation. She had no idea how long she would be staying, and it was the first time she had been without friends her own age.

Hannah stayed well back from the crowd. To the cheers of bicyclists and pedestrians, the first car left through the bow door, up the concrete ramp to the street beyond. She was in no hurry. The thought of meeting her great-aunt Caroline made her very uneasy. She still blamed her stepmother for sending her to stay with a relative she had never met. Her father would never have sent her away if it had been up to him.

There was no cooling sea breeze now that the ship had docked. The air was thick with exhaust fumes, and the damp heat made Hannah's hair sag limply. Her shirt was clinging to her slim body by the time she followed the stream of excited passengers off the ferry. The suitcase banged against her leg as she walked along the pier. Several people were waiting behind the sturdy barrier marking the end of the dock. There were frantic waves and eager meetings, but not for her. Mrs. Chase, her great-aunt, had written her to go to the waiting room of the terminal, so Hannah followed the signs to a long covered walkway.

On one of the huge round wooden piles sat a herring gull, inquisitively following her movements with an icy blue eye. Hannah was sure it would fly away at the last moment, but it did not. She passed within a foot of it, close enough to see the red tip of its bill.

The waiting room was not air-conditioned; two fans whirled noisily, stirring discarded pieces of paper and dust. Hannah glanced anxiously around her. Nobody greeted her, so she put the suitcase down and sat on one of the blue plastic chairs and closed her eyes.

Ten minutes passed. Then, with a quickening of her senses, Hannah knew she was being observed. Opening her eyes, she saw that a woman was staring at her. Hannah's heart sank. The woman was dressed in a baggy black dress. Above a narrow, pointed chin, her face was wrinkled and tanned like leather, and her gray, strawlike hair was pulled into a tight bun. She had a blunt, knobbly nose and a disapproving stare.

Surely this wasn't her Aunt Caroline. Hannah's heart sank; she could read no welcoming sign in the thin lips or the dark eyes that glittered fiercely from deep within the folds of skin.

6

"Aunt—" began Hannah.

"I'm Mrs. Donohue," the woman interrupted her, speaking with just a touch of an Irish brogue. "I work for your aunt. Housekeeper and dogsbody. Give me the suitcase, haven't got all day." Stretching out a hand with long, bony fingers, she took Hannah's suitcase and headed abruptly for the exit.

Outside the sun was blinding and the air smelled sharply of salt, fish, and tar. Mrs. Donohue examined the suitcase critically. "Good leather," she commented, reaching for the rear door of a large Buick station wagon. The latch was stuck and Mrs. Donohue had to rattle it forcibly before the door swung open. As if nothing had happened, she placed the case in the back and continued. "Can't abide that fancy stuff they have now. Parachute luggage!" With this she took the driver's seat as Hannah scrambled in next to her, fumbling with her seat belt. "This car was the last year they used real metal; won't touch one of those tin cans they sell now. Your aunt has a Cadillac; I won't drive it."

Mrs. Donohue didn't seem to expect any reply, and Hannah was grateful. She hoped her mistake would soon be forgotten. How could she have been so foolish as to think Mrs. Donohue was Mrs. Chase? Her father didn't talk much about his only aunt, but he had mentioned that she was elegant and cultured and very rich.

There was a hive of activity around the steamship wharf. She had expected a New England village of the kind seen in history books, but Vineyard Haven had little charm. She had never seen so many utility poles or signs saying Wrong Way and Do Not Enter. Hannah caught glimpses of the town through the traffic. There was an A & P, a drugstore, restaurants, souvenir shops, a boutique, and several fish markets.

Mrs. Donohue paid no attention to other drivers. "Won't

win a beauty contest, this place," she commented as they inched forward. "Used to be a quiet little town." She paused, then added with a sniff, "Before the war."

However, once out of the business area the Buick picked up speed, and Hannah saw more fashionable houses, many nestled behind picket fences with climbing roses growing up walls or forming red and white arches over garden gates.

The road gradually rose, and on the right Hannah saw a great stretch of water sparkling in the sunlight. Moments later, the pavement dipped, and she could see nothing on either side but tall, straight-sided hedgerows, clipped neatly along the sides and top.

Mrs. Donohue drove with both hands tightly on the steering wheel and her back straight, peering ahead like a student driver. Hannah smiled, despite her weariness. She thought of last year when she and Melanie had taken driver's ed. Melanie approached the task as she did everything else: with bravado. Her favorite phrase was "There's nothing either good or bad but thinking makes it so." Whirling confidently around the practice course, she tried to insert a cassette into the player and drove the Ford Escort into the huge mountain of tires that was meant to represent a truck. Sitting there with the instructor next to her and Hannah in the back, Melanie watched as the last of the tires solemnly bounced off the car hood and wobbled across the lot. Then she said with a bright smile, "We're fine, but look at the truck." She did not get her permit.

"We're going up-island," said Mrs. Donohue in her abrupt manner. "Your aunt lives on the far side of the Vineyard." Scowling as three girls on mopeds swerved dangerously around them, she added, "Where there aren't any crowds." After that, nothing was said as they drove steadily west. The scenery became more rural, and the road ahead was a black ribbon of asphalt.

The Buick crested a rise. Now they were driving directly into the setting sun; the afternoon light glinted on the windshield, rendering it virtually opaque. The road dipped, and a thick mist swirled around them. Huge drifts streamed up from the ocean, as if sucked into a vacuum, and wove themselves around the station wagon, thick as cotton. For an instant Hannah could see nothing. It was as if she were riding inside a cloud.

Suddenly the road ahead was not empty. The mist vanished and with a clarity that astonished her, she saw a horse-drawn cart, moving slowly in front of them.

An old woman sat slumped in a corner of the cart. Around her neck hung a sign bearing the single word *WITCH*. On each side trudged two men dressed as Puritans, followed by a crowd of similarly dressed villagers. There was no sound. A patient donkey pulled the cart; it would not be hurried by the driver flicking its reins.

The donkey stopped beneath a huge oak; a blacksmith's forge glowed red nearby. As Hannah watched in horror, the two men dragged the witch from the cart, ripping the dress from her shoulder. The blacksmith pumped his bellows and then from the coals he drew a branding iron, the letter W, cherry red at its tip. Hannah was aware of a tremendous heat passing in front of her face. Instinctively she pressed her head back into the seat.

Passing the iron once in front of the witch's face so she could feel its heat, the smith aimed it directly at her shoulder and pressed against the skin.

The witch screamed; the noise frightened many of the onlookers, who turned their faces away. A strong smell of burning flesh filled the air. She was dragged, moaning in agony, toward a great tree. The donkey stood rigidly still, only its tail swishing lazily. A rope was expertly tossed over a bough of the tree, and a noose fashioned at one end.

The prisoner was hauled to her feet. The noose was tightened around her neck.

The villagers gathered around in a semicircle, adults and children alike. The witch's eyes spit fire.

The driver gave a sharp tug on the rein and urged the donkey forward. The witch swung at the end of the rope, her black boots kicking below her dress.

Hannah jerked upright in her seat, looking wildly around her. The vision had vanished, and the mist too. Mrs. Donohue was still gazing directly ahead, hands clenched on the wheel. Hannah shook her head. I must have dozed off, she thought, moving uneasily in her seat. Pins and needles shot through one foot, and she reached down to massage it. Just at that moment a large brown rabbit shot into the road ahead of them. Mrs. Donohue slammed the brakes on; she and Hannah were flung violently from side to side as the station wagon slid into the sand alongside the road, fishtailed, and then came to a halt in a cloud of sand and dust.

For Hannah it was as if the past three years had been swallowed up in an instant. Gritting her teeth and closing her eyes, she suppressed a scream. It all came back to her—the boy darting in front of her father's Honda, the instantaneous reaction. Frantically he'd turned the wheel, the tires screeching. Then everything seemed to move in slow motion. The rear of the Honda hit the curb and was lifted off the ground. Then came the sickening thud as they slammed up against a tree. Finally there was a dreadful silence broken only by the hissing of steam from the crushed radiator.

It had taken nearly an hour to cut her mother from the wreckage. Hannah caught the quick shake of the head the paramedic gave to the state trooper. And she knew.

Hannah had fought to see her mother, but the trooper held her back. There wasn't one last chance, one final opportunity to say things that should have been said. Her mother was dead. All around had been confusion, and the wailing of sirens. And one endless sadness.

There would be no one with whom to take slow, summer-evening walks around the block. No one to confide in. Nobody just to be with.

Seat belts had saved Hannah and her father, but not her mother. The boy who caused the accident was never found. Hannah still blamed him, though she knew that was irrational.

"It's all right, girl," said Mrs. Donohue. "Just a jackrabbit, island's full of them."

"I'm sorry," Hannah said miserably, still gripping her seat. "I didn't expect . . . I guess I was asleep."

Mrs. Donohue patted Hannah's hand with her bony fingers. "Don't worry. As they say, 'Worse things happen at sea,' girl."

Hannah managed a weak smile as they turned into a graveled lane; above, the trees closed together, cutting out most of the light. "Stewart's Lane," said Mrs. Donohue with relish. "Your aunt owns it and all the land around here including the beach; she wouldn't give those developers the time of day. She's the richest woman on the island, and she tells them where to get off."

They were coming to the end of the lane. A large pond on the left had a solitary white swan floating serenely on it. Then they had a brief uninterrupted view out to sea. Yachts

11

with bright, billowing sails ran before the wind, and squat little lobster boats methodically followed trap lines. "It's beautiful," Hannah murmured.

"Hmm! Vineyard Sound. It's beautiful, all right," said Mrs. Donohue. "But don't forget it's treacherous. There's many a widow still alive on the island waiting for the sea to give up its dead."

"What about my great-aunt?" asked Hannah, her eyes still fixed on the ocean. "How did her husband die?"

"Nothing romantic there, girl. He had a heart attack in his office in New York. Made millions. That's how he bought Stewart's Grove."

"Stewart's Grove." Hannah turned to look at Mrs. Donohue. "The house has a name?"

"And a history. Stewarts owned it for generations. The original building was partly made from a Puritan farm. Its timbers and stone were used in the old kitchens. Saved money."

Mrs. Donohue turned off the road and crossed a narrow stone bridge over a stream. Then she continued as if there had been no break in the conversation. "Everyone, starting with Captain Stewart, added something. Now"—she shook her head in disgust—"the historical commission people won't let you touch anything over twenty years old. Years ago some rich banker named Dalby bought it. He added Long Walk and the north wing, where your aunt lives. I stay in Tisbury. He was crazy. People called it Dalby's Folly. Then ..." Mrs. Donohue hesitated, shifted gears, and became silent.

"Then what?" asked Hannah, intrigued.

"He stayed here one night. Next day his body washed up on the beach. They said his face was twisted with a look of sheer terror. His hair was supposed to have turned white. Don't believe a word of it," she added with a loud sniff. "People do have to talk. Don't pay any attention to rumors, myself. Believe in facing facts, particularly the unpleasant ones. Well, Stewart's Grove was almost a ruin when your great-uncle bought it. Cost three million to restore—when a million was a million. Soon after that he died. Some silly people say the place is jinxed. More fool them!" she retorted, pressing her foot on the accelerator and throwing Hannah back in her seat. They shot up a slight hill, scattering sand on both sides of the car.

In the distance, rising slowly into view, was the outline of a huge stone building. It seemed to shimmer in the sunlight. Without any warning, without any reason, Hannah was seized with an overwhelming sense of foreboding. An involuntary shudder ran up her spine. And a chill settled in every limb.

First Night

HANNAH SHIVERED DESPITE HERSELF. "NONSENSE," she said firmly.

Mrs. Donohue looked at her. "What is?"

"Oh, nothing," replied Hannah, confused. "Nothing." She knew it was an optical illusion, something to do with the angle of the driveway and her own nervous apprehension at the end of a long, tiring journey.

Stewart's Grove was made of sandstone, a yellow ocher color that caught the sun and shone like gold. A short wing was set at right angles to a longer one. Narrow, deep-set windows revealed two stories and attics beneath the steep slate roof. The line of the roof was interrupted by gables painted black, and where the wings connected rose thin brick chimneys, each topped by four chimney pots.

The drive was narrow; the Buick's tires crunched on gravel, and the windshield and sides of the vehicle were occasionally slapped by branches of lilacs. Mrs. Donohue ignored them and charged ahead.

At the end of the driveway, Hannah caught sight of a dark blue Cadillac parked in front of a stone staircase leading to wooden double doors. The foot of the stairs was guarded by a pair of sandstone lions. Mrs. Donohue, however, forked left.

"This is the west wing; your aunt closed most of it off years ago," commented Mrs. Donohue, switching the ignition off. "This was the old luggage entrance; now it's used instead of the main doors. Out you go."

Hannah did as she was told, glad to stretch her legs. In front of her was a wide lawn, at its center a huge marble fountain with a statue of a Greek god waving a trident and carrying a giant fish under his arm. There wasn't any water.

"Silliest thing I ever saw," said Mrs. Donohue, following her gaze. "Came all the way from France, that did. It's what you'd expect from there."

The old wing was long, and atop the parapet was a series of life-size statues of Roman emperors, three of whom had lost their heads. Beyond the building, near the cliff's edge, was a huge oak tree.

"Stewart's Oak," said Mrs. Donohue. "Planted a hundred fifty years ago. Ninety feet tall if it's an inch. Roots destroyed the tennis court—not that anyone plays tennis. Used to be dozens of them. They were cut down for timber fifty years ago."

A man hurried around the far end of the house. He wore an old brown jacket, a pair of stained khaki trousers, and a battered, green felt hat, which he took from his head as he drew close.

15

Taking Hannah's hand, he smiled, wiping the sweat off his brow with a sleeve. "So this is Hannah, eh?"

Hannah saw that the green threads on his shirt were grass cuttings.

"My husband, Mr. Donohue," said his wife shortly, starting up the short flight of steps that led to the luggage entrance. "Bring her luggage."

"I'm the gardener," he added, rather unnecessarily. "And the odd-job man." Sensing the warmth of his personality, Hannah liked him immediately.

Following the two women, Hannah's suitcase in hand, he added, "Mrs. Chase will be glad to see you. She doesn't have much company these days." Mrs. Donohue let out a loud sniff as if any information about their employer were privileged. By the door was a large stone vase with a shrub in it. The housekeeper stopped and pointed. "See the stone pot with that plant—"

"Podocarpus," her husband added, almost apologetically giving Hannah a secret wink.

"—with that fern pine in it. Well, we keep a key in it for emergencies." Pushing the gray-blue leaves aside, she showed Hannah a key. "During the day the door isn't locked, so you won't need a key. Come on." She pushed the heavy door open; its bottom edge scraped against the stone flags of the floor. Dark green paint had flaked off, exposing the brown beneath. "Here we are. Mr. Donohue will take the case to your room." Her husband grinned and left them, obeying her command.

Although she was tired, Hannah looked about her with interest. The entrance hall was small. There was a small round table beside a coat tree. Directly before them a narrow oak staircase led to the floor above. The newels were carved into the shapes of mythological creatures. A griffin with folded wings glared at her.

Hannah was surprised to discover an elevator. Mrs. Donohue opened the gates. They entered; it wasn't very big, little more than a cage, and it made a series of protesting sounds as they slowly rose to the next floor. The housekeeper controlled it with a handle, and when they stopped, Hannah had to step down to the floor.

"Mr. Chase had the elevator installed," Mrs. Donohue informed Hannah, "though why the servants couldn't carry luggage up the stairs is beyond me." She led the way swiftly across a landing and into a large room containing glass-fronted cupboards filled with china. Beyond was a small kitchen. Walking quickly through, they entered a dining room. On the wall above the fireplace were two portraits, each life size.

"Your aunt and Mr. Chase," she said without breaking her step. "Before the war."

Mrs. Chase would then have been in her twenties, thought Hannah. She wore a formal white gown that emphasized a striking high-boned face almost olive in color. Her full lips were parted in a slight smile. Rich black hair was styled high on her forehead like a crown. In some magical way, the artist had caught her eyes. They were deep set and dark and gazed intently at the world from the canvas.

Then Hannah entered a bright, cheerful room with a high ceiling. The furniture seemed to consist entirely of antiques. French windows, leading to a balcony with a view of Vineyard Sound, were wide open. One wall was lined with bookshelves filled with leather-bound volumes.

Mrs. Chase sat on a long sofa, reading the *New Yorker*. By her side was a butler's tray with a china teapot and a single

17

cup. As her aunt rose to her feet, Hannah realized she was a tall woman, nearly six feet tall. She was older, of course, than in her portrait; her hair was white. However, her eyes had lost none of their piercing quality; there was authority in her face.

Her aunt held out a hand. "So you are Hannah," she said, smiling briefly and, Hannah thought, without warmth.

She took Mrs. Chase's hand. It was cold and almost translucent.

"You are welcome, child," Mrs. Chase added gravely. Without looking at Mrs. Donohue she said, "More tea, please, and some sandwiches."

Picking up the tea tray, Mrs. Donohue left.

Mrs. Chase was studying Hannah, who felt like an insect under a microscope. "I had expected you to be tall like your father. Never mind. It will be difficult for you here," her great-aunt continued. "I live alone and value privacy, and for that reason there is no telephone. I spend all my time attempting to keep Stewart's Grove in a manner my husband would have wanted. His investments need constant supervision. I have learned to live a solitary life; guests do tend to upset an established routine."

"Oh, but I . . ."

Mrs. Chase shook her head; it was a delicate but commanding movement. "Your father is my nephew and my only living relative. I felt it to be my duty to assist him; after all, he travels a great deal. And there is, of course"—she paused—"the problem of his new wife."

Hannah nodded miserably. How could her father have forgotten her mother so soon? Gayle wasn't even very attractive. She was tall and thin and had mousy hair. Even now Hannah found it unbelievable.

"Sit, child."

Hannah perched on the edge of the sofa. There was a painful silence.

Mrs. Donohue returned with the tea tray, some thinly sliced sandwiches, cookies, and a second cup. She placed them on the butler's tray and left the room.

Mrs. Chase leaned forward and poured two steaming cups of tea. "Help yourself to cream and sugar, Hannah, and sandwiches if you wish."

They spent the next thirty minutes in small talk, which Hannah found exhausting. She'd become very adept at concealing her feelings, and she did not wish to be a burden to her great-aunt. On the other hand, she hadn't wanted to be packed off to some old relative miles from anywhere without any idea of when she could go home. It wasn't fair. Her father said he couldn't leave Hannah alone when he went on business trips with his new wife until he was sure she would take care of herself. It wasn't her fault she'd been ill. Hannah wanted to make a good impression on Mrs. Chase, but her aunt and she had nothing in common.

Just when she felt she must scream from the tension, her aunt, realizing the futility of further conversation, said, "Well, my dear, you must be very tired. I'll take you to your room."

Rising, she led the way to the double doors, and they walked the length of the central hall.

Her aunt did not use the elevator; she walked past the dinner-service room and led the way down the staircase.

"The house is very large," replied Hannah, wanting to say something and hurrying to keep up. "I don't think I'll ever learn my way around."

"Well, perhaps you won't have to," said her aunt at the foot of the stairs. "Your first appointment with this psychiatrist, Dr. Marsh, is tomorrow at ten. I did not tell Mrs. Do-nohue about your illness—you're recovered now, and she is not likely to understand the complexities of the condition. Soon you can go home to your father."

She doesn't want me either, thought Hannah unhappily. Well, I don't want to be here. I'd rather be home in Ohio with my friends—if they even remember me.

"I shut off all the rooms in the west wing once my butler, McGlynn, retired," Mrs. Chase said, pointing to the set of double doors to her left. "But his quarters did have a shower and other facilities, so I told Mrs. Donohue to open them up." She walked quickly down the hall away from the doors. "Here is the butler's pantry, which McGlynn made into his bed-sitting room."

When Hannah followed her aunt through the door, she gasped. It was the most masculine-looking room she had ever been in. Then, seeing the humor of it, she was overcome with an irresistible urge to laugh, which she tried desperately to stifle and then change into a sneeze. Her friend Melanie's favorite word summed it up: tacky. There was an empty gun rack, a stand for fishing tackle, and a carpet whose threadbare colors had faded into one rusty brown. The wallpaper was light green with tiny spouting whales in neat rows a foot apart. There really wasn't much paper visible, however, for the walls were crammed with pictures of stern gentlemen in full beards and with what appeared to be framed photographs of famous paintings. One was *The Last Supper*, but Christ and some of his disciples had almost faded away.

"My butler's taste was, shall we say, eclectic," said Mrs. Chase, looking about her. "He was Irish, you know."

The bed was a four-poster with a dark red canopy over it. Hannah could not imagine why the butler had chosen any-

20

thing so bizarre. The next-largest item was a wardrobe made of a light-colored wood with long mirrors in each door and four drawers beneath with painted glass handles. One of the mirrors had lost its silvering and was little more than plain glass.

Mrs. Chase followed her gaze. "He was very old when he retired," she said, by way of explanation. "The room is not to my taste, but it will serve. Through that door"—she pointed—"is the bathroom. Do you want a scale to weigh on?"

Hannah shook her head. "No. I can judge."

By the bed were her suitcase and a trunk that had been shipped directly from Reach Out. A week ago the whole dormitory had been filled with the bustling excitement of packing. Melanie had kept a brave face on it. "You're out of here," she had said, throwing an armload of clothes into the trunk. "Me next." For Hannah's sake, she had tried to sound carefree. In the end, they'd both had to sit on the trunk to get it closed.

"I'm really going to miss you," Hannah had said. "You're the one who wants to leave, not me. I'm not going anywhere, just to some old aunt I've never met. I won't like it there."

"Now just stop that," Melanie had commanded. "What did Dr. Wilbanks tell you about listening to that little voice? You have to keep the faith. Don't worry about me, there'll be a whole bunch of new girls next week—all of them sent here by mistake. I'll still be the mother superior." But it was one of the few times Hannah had seen a tear in her friend's eye. Melanie had been at Reach Out longer than any girl. Her violent mood swings appeared to be a thing of the past, but the doctors wanted to be sure she could cope before they sent her home.

21

Standing with her hand on the knob, Mrs. Chase asked, "Do you want anything to eat later or would you prefer to retire?"

"I'm kind of tired...."

"Well then ... breakfast is at nine. Mrs. Donohue will come for you. Good night, child." And she left without looking back.

Hannah was thankful to be left alone. Digging into the trunk, she took out her hair dryer and a cassette player wrapped tightly inside her souvenir towel from the dorm. There were a dozen cassette tapes in a plastic bag, and Hannah took out Melanie's favorite, *Whitesnake,* and slipped it into the player.

It was funny, she and Melanie were nothing alike, and yet they had become close friends. Melanie had a huge collection of cassette tapes, and soon Hannah had become familiar with a score of rock groups she'd never heard before. They discussed books and found a common interest in music. And when they felt crazy, they used Melanie's blow dryer, mousse, and a curling iron to produce wild and wacky hairdos.

From the trunk she took a photograph of herself and Melanie, carefully wrapped in tissue paper. It was a gag photo. They had decided to imitate the models posing in an advertisement in *Sassy.* Melanie, wearing a big red bow headband, had taken the picture with a ten-second delay but had tripped scrambling back to get in the picture. They had just had time to put on the silly pouting look of the models before the flash went off. The picture captured them just before they collapsed, rolling hysterically on the floor. She closed the trunk and opened the suitcase.

Lying facedown was a Cabbage Patch doll, a gift from

Melanie. It was called "Grumps," the nickname Melanie had given Mrs. Pascoe, the school librarian. Melanie was her aide, and the librarian suspected, quite correctly, that Melanie never charged fines for late or lost books. All a girl had to do was tell Melanie she'd lost a book, and the card disappeared. If the book turned up, Melanie typed up a new card and scuffed it in the dust to age it.

The tape had reached "Is This Love?" Hannah propped Grumps comfortably in one of the corners of the window seat in front of heavy green drapes and looked around the room, shaking her head. In this little world McGlynn had lived alone and virtually unneeded. What possible use could Mrs. Chase have for a butler? In a way it was sad. Her aunt was living alone in this great house, dreaming of the past and cherishing the memory of a dead husband.

Then she realized with a start that this was really what she herself was doing. Hannah had been angry at her father because he could put the past behind him and get on with his life and she couldn't.

As if to distract herself, Hannah opened the other door to her room. She peered into the dark hall beyond. To the left was a pile of furniture blocking the way to the main wing. To the right the hall stretched into the gloom. She took a few paces and could see the set of double doors leading to the old wing. Suddenly she felt herself shivering and was grateful to return to her bedroom.

Tired though she was, Hannah spent the next quarter of an hour unpacking. Her T-shirts, shorts, and underwear went into the top bureau drawer, and she hung her winter things and her single dress from the metal hangers in the wardrobe. At the back of the wardrobe, she discovered a glass bell jar with a mounted pheasant in it. Its beady eyes glittered in the light. For a second, its eyes seemed to hold hers. The glass jar shimmered; the eyes burned into her head. The stare was hypnotic. Only an enormous effort made it possible to turn away. "That's enough of you," she said, putting the pheasant in the corner, facing the wall.

Next she took her toilet items into the bathroom. Whatever its original purpose, it had not been intended as a bathroom, as it was no more than five feet wide. There was an empty medicine cabinet and a sink. Hannah found an electric outlet for the curling comb the girls had given her when she left Reach Out. Deciding to skip a shower, she sponged off with a cool washcloth. Then, feeling much refreshed, she combed out her hair and put a cotton nightshirt on.

From the side pocket of the case Hannah took the framed picture of her parents. Putting it on her bedside table, she studied it closely. Her mother had been beautiful. At the time of her death, wrinkles were beginning to show, and perhaps the eyes were a little tired, but the original beauty was there for all to see. She didn't believe it when people said they looked alike, not even when they pointed out the identical rich brown of their hair or the tiny cleft in their chins. For eighteen years her father had been married to her mother. Then how, a year after her death, could he forget her and marry his secretary, Gayle? When Hannah reproached him, he could only say he was in love. Her mother had shared all his early struggles, and now that he was a successful engineer, another woman was trying to take her place.

For her appointment with Dr. Marsh, Hannah put out the better pair of jeans and a cotton sweater with big, bold, black and white stripes. If she could find them in the morning, she would wear the matching earrings.

Before getting into bed, Hannah pulled back the heavy

drapes across her window. Directly in front of her was a formal garden. Beyond the cliffs the sky was streaked with gold, and beneath, the ocean reflected the last of the sun.

Hannah folded the quilt back and slid between the sheets. The mattress felt a little damp and lumpy, but it was so good to rest at last that she barely noticed. With her head on the pillow, she could hear the rumble of the ocean surf in the distance. She felt herself drifting, falling, out of control.

Hannah slept. Beyond Stewart's Grove the sky darkened to black. The moon and stars were masked by cloud.

In Vineyard Sound the waves rose, crested, and then fell on the beach, driving forward until forced to retreat and leaving long, thin fingers of seaweed behind. A fox trotted along the edge of the cliff, barked, and receiving an answering call from his mate, sought her in the shelter of the trees north of the great house.

Deep in the recesses of the unused old building something stirred. A shadow grew in darkness, twisted, divided, and re-formed. It was on the move. The room was icy cold, as if the life were being sucked out of it. Tendrils of shadow curled over and around objects, and slipped under the door. The shadow grew luminescent; its center pulsated.

It left the bakehouse, slid around corners, making its way to Long Walk, a great hall stretching nearly the length of the west wing. There it paused, then slipped noiselessly over the dusty oak floors, leaving no trace of its passing, until it was at Hannah's bedroom.

The shape remained motionless outside the door. In her sleep Hannah moved restlessly, muttering something unintelligible. She pulled the blanket around her as the room became cold.

When the shadow came into the room, it was still un-formed.

It might have had arms or legs, there may have been the suggestion of a head, of a long black dress, of a pale, pale face. There might have been a sound, a low, pitiful sob, but there was no one to hear. It might have swirled around the four-poster bed as if noting the presence of someone new.

After a time the presence returned the way it had come. It left the bedroom and undulated along the short passage to the double doors. Here it hesitated, but only for an instant. The luminescence faded, but beyond the doors it reformed and slowly made its way down Long Walk. But its movements seemed to have more purpose. It had found what it sought.

3
Dr. Marsh

THE NEXT MORNING HANNAH AWOKE TO A WHIS-
tling sound. At first it seemed at the back of her consciousness, part of a dream. Then she gradually became aware that
she was in a strange bed, in a room she didn't know. There
was a moment of panic; then she was awake, and the sound
was not within her but outside. It seemed to come from the
window. There she found an old-fashioned speaking tube
hidden by the drapes. Hannah had seen them in movies. Removing the top, she placed the tube to her ear.

"Can you find your way up?" demanded Mrs. Donohue
from a long way off.

"I think so," replied Hannah, speaking into the tube and
feeling a bit silly. Then she put the tube to her ear, but if
Mrs. Donohue bothered to reply, Hannah never heard her.

There was no time to shower: it wouldn't do to be late. A

mad search of the suitcase finally turned up the missing earring in the crease at the back.

As she left, Hannah took one last look in the mirror doors of the wardrobe. There was a tightness about her mouth and there were shadows behind her eyes. She wouldn't be innocent again; too much had happened. "A sadder and a wiser kiddo," Melanie had pronounced after her first month at Reach Out.

Outside the room she paused briefly to get her bearings. Hannah remembered that the butler's pantry was directly beneath the dining room, and once she discovered the stairs the rest was easy. The elevator was closer, but somehow she didn't feel comfortable taking it.

To her surprise there was no one in the breakfast room. A mahogany table, with a huge vase of fresh-cut flowers as its centerpiece, was set for one. However, there were a pot of coffee and several strips of bacon and scrambled eggs in a silver chafing dish, and two slices of rye toast.

Wondering whether she should begin alone, Hannah was interrupted by Mrs. Donohue. "Eat up, girl," she said, entering from the central hall. "Haven't got all day. Your aunt finished hours ago." Hannah no longer felt sick at the sight of food, but her anxiety at the prospect of meeting Dr. Marsh took away her appetite, and she left most of her food untouched.

In the Buick, Mrs. Donohue asked, "This Dr. Marsh. Have you ever met her?"

"No. My doctor knew her."

"She lives in a nice part of town. They can afford to, can't they? Course, I don't hold much with psychiatrists. Stands to reason you can't cure anything just by talking. We didn't have them . . . before the war."

Their journey took them along the main road to Edgartown, by the edge of a giant pine forest. The ocean was to their right, but after a few miles a mist coming up from the water swirled around the station wagon, thickening and then thinning. Mrs. Donohue was irritated at having to slow down. Then, abruptly, the fog vanished. The sun was shining and the sky cloudless. *How odd,* thought Hannah, remembering the strange dream she'd had the day of her arrival. *These fogs just seem to come out of . . .*

"Don't say much, do you?"

Hannah started. "Gee, I was just thinking how quickly the mist disappeared. One minute it was there . . ."

Mrs. Donohue wrenched the gearshift; there was the familiar grinding noise. "Pooh!" she snorted. "That was nothing. Sometimes it's so thick it's like breathing wet cotton."

At the outskirts of town, traffic was already blocking every road and lane. "Damn off-islanders," muttered Mrs. Donohue. "Wasn't like this . . ."

"Before the war," muttered Hannah, under her breath. Then she blushed, surprised at her boldness.

Finally they reached the harbor. Mrs. Donohue pulled up in front of a fire hydrant. "It's useless trying to go any farther," she said. "North Water Street is through there," she added, pointing, "and Light House View is a short street to the right."

Hannah scrambled out just as a police patrol car began moving toward the station wagon. Before she could ask what she should do about the return trip, Mrs. Donohue had disappeared down a side road.

The sidewalks were thronged with people. They all looked so happy, and she was on her way to see a shrink. Why? She knew she had been wrong to stop eating. Above all, she didn't want some old man in a suit telling her why she felt the way she did. Dr. Wilbanks was nice, but he was too easygoing and pleasant. He probably never raised his voice to one of his patients. Anyway, how could he know what it was like to lose your mother and have your father marry someone who wasn't even remotely as interesting?

Thinking about her father and stepmother made Hannah pass the house she was looking for, and she had to retrace her steps. It was large and dominated by a huge porch whose roof was supported by great wooden pillars. Except for plum-colored shutters, the whole building was painted white. In front was a garden full of irises of every color: purple, red, orange, white, and gold. A huge linden tree near the walkway provided welcome shade.

A short flight of brick steps, flanked by intricate wrought-iron railings, led to the porch, and sitting on the steps was a large tabby cat eyeing her curiously, its glass-green eyes following her every move.

At the last moment, arching its back, it made a leap toward her. Hannah took a step backward. The cat, still watching her, moved slowly aside, then sprang effortlessly onto a cracked birdbath. There it remained, one leg hanging over the edge.

The front door was of solid oak with a bell set in its frame. However, there was a piece of Scotch tape over the button and a card with Walk In roughly printed in careless letters.

The hall was cool. At the end, to her right, an area had been screened off. A large hand-lettered sign in the same scrawl proclaimed Waiting Room.

Feeling uncomfortably hot and regretting having worn a sweater, Hannah went behind the screen; there were a chair and a table covered with magazines. The room was not air-conditioned, and the thought of looking at an old *National Geographic* was boring.

"Read the one on Uranus," said a cheerful female voice behind her. "It's a classic. All those rings."

Hannah turned quickly. Dr. Marsh was a short woman dressed in jeans and a sweatshirt at least three sizes too big with Edgartown Regatta written on it and a sketch of several sailboats below. She was smiling broadly. In her right hand was a gardening trowel. Placing the trowel on the table, she stuck out her hand. "I'm Lucetta Marsh." Hannah took her hand. Dr. Marsh's eye fell on the magazine again. "Or is it Saturn? Whatever. We aren't going there." She peered over the top of her half-moon glasses as if trying to get a better look.

Hannah tried not to stare at the doctor, who certainly wasn't what she had expected. At Reach Out, Dr. Wilbanks always wore a suit and tie. Melanie said she felt as if she were talking to a priest. You always felt guilty even if you didn't know why.

"Come on out of this heat."

Hannah followed her down a flight of stairs.

"This is the consulting room," announced Dr. Marsh, opening a door and ushering her in. "It's cooler here."

Hannah looked around curiously. There were stacks of papers everywhere, some tied together with twine. One wall was devoted entirely to bookshelves, but there were dozens of books piled in various corners, on chairs, and on the floor. *What a mess,* she thought.

"Bit of a mess, isn't it?" said the doctor.

Hannah gave a guilty start and tried to look elsewhere.

31

The opposite wall was a huge set of French doors, and outside was a forest of miniature trees in clay pots.

"Bonsai," said Dr. Marsh. "Go and look if you like."

Opening one of the doors, Hannah stepped outside. Dr. Marsh followed her.

"Always been fascinated by the Far East," she continued. "A very patient people. We can learn a lot from them. See that one there?"

Hannah looked at a ragged stump with scaly bark.

"Ugly brute, isn't it?" said the doctor, proudly. "It's a western juniper, over a hundred years old. You can make a dwarf tree out of any plant. That one there is a creeping fig."

The garden was a remarkable sight. There was a wooden deck and beyond a miniature granite bridge spanning a small fishpond. A steady trickle of water came from a bamboo spout nestled among rocks at the pool's edge.

"The Japanese place great value on nature, but they live in crowded conditions," she continued, "so they perfected a way of duplicating nature on a small scale. Sometimes a gull flies in; then you lose all sense of proportion. It looks as big as an elephant. Here endeth the lesson on dwarf trees. Let's go back in, shall we?"

In the consulting room, they sat down on either side of a small folding table on which lay a manila folder and four neatly stacked packets of Wrigley's sugarless gum. Dr. Marsh took the top one and carefully slid a stick out. As if she were just now remembering Hannah's presence, she offered the packet to her. Hannah shook her head.

"Coffee? I can make chocolate."

"No, thank you."

"Let's just talk, shall we?"

Hannah nodded. The doctor's voice had a definite New York City accent.

"Everyone's got problems. Some seem worse than others." She peered at Hannah over the top of her glasses. "Right?"

"I guess so."

"No guess about it, Hannah. Lot of suffering out there. The trick's to get it in perspective." Dr. Marsh picked up the file from the table. "What I like about referrals is we don't have to fill out all those files the state of Massachusetts is so fussy about."

Hannah nodded, feeling some response was needed.

Dr. Marsh flicked through the pages inside the folder, her reading glasses perched on her nose.

"At five foot five, you got down to ninety-eight pounds, huh?"

"Yes."

The psychiatrist closed the folder and tossed it onto the table. She carefully unwrapped a fresh stick of gum. "You know, I don't tend to beat about the bush. Maybe I'm too pushy, but long silences unnerve me. First meetings are always a bit sticky," she said, getting to her feet. Rubbing her hands on her jeans, she added, "Why don't we take a walk? You can see something of the harbor, and we can start to get acquainted. What do you say?"

"Okay." It wasn't really a question. Hannah took her purse and followed the doctor up the stairs.

On the front porch, Dr. Marsh stopped. "Just look at Sigmund," she said in exasperation, glaring at the tabby. "He lies in that empty birdbath thinking birds will fly in while he's there. That cat is crazy."

"It isn't very logical," said Hannah as Sigmund licked a paw and scrubbed behind his ear.

Dr. Marsh rubbed the cat under its chin; the purring was very loud. "That's why we have psychiatrists," she said. "To study the illogical side of our natures."

A narrow flight of wooden steps dropped steeply toward the harbor. "I'll lead the way," she said.

At the bottom was a bench. They sat without speaking. A boat near the lighthouse was winching a lobster trap up. Gulls whirled around in a frenzy. To their right a small ferry carrying a Jeep and a van crossed the narrow strip of water that separated the Vineyard from Chappaquiddick Island. For a moment it seemed they wouldn't be able to hear each other for the screeching of sea gulls as they dived and rose, triumphant or disappointed, around the crab shacks. The air was warm and moist, and the smell of salt water sharp and distinct.

Hannah looked out at the boats tied along the dock. Each had a name, usually a woman's. One was called *Saucy Nancy* and another *Mae Bee*.

"Herman Melville sailed from here," said Dr. Marsh, looking out into the harbor entrance. "When he returned he wrote *Moby-Dick*. If he hadn't been a writer, he would have been a great shrink." Then she turned to Hannah and said, "How was it at Reach Out?"

"It was great."

Dr. Marsh grinned. "That bad, huh?"

Hannah smiled too, but it was partly because she remembered what Melanie had said about *Moby-Dick*: "If you like stories about men with one leg chasing whales, my dear, this is for you."

"It was at first. Then I made friends. First Melanie, then Laura and Dori. The others called us the Four Musketeers. Melanie is still there; the rest of us are free."

Dr. Marsh looked closely at Hannah. Her eyes seemed to be looking right into the girl. "Yes, free. Tell me about Melanie."

"She always wore the neatest clothes and liked wearing this headband with a large red bow just above the forehead. She also wore great big endless earrings. Oh God—" Hannah broke off. "I miss her."

Dr. Marsh put an arm around her as Hannah fumbled in her purse for a Kleenex. She blew her nose and added, "Miss Johnson, the principal, was not amused at the way she dressed."

"Not amused?"

"That was another of Melanie's phrases. Apparently Queen Victoria said it all the time in England."

Dr. Marsh was smiling.

"We could tell each other anything. We were our sister's keepers."

"Another of Melanie's phrases?"

"Yes."

Conversation became easier as the time passed; Hannah told Dr. Marsh the whole story of her mother's death, her father's remarriage, and her own attempt to starve herself to death. The doctor barely interrupted her, merely nodding encouragement when Hannah faltered.

At the end of the hour they walked back to the house, making an appointment for Wednesday. Sigmund was still lying in the birdbath. Hannah stroked him between the ears. Then she walked to the end of William Street and saw the parked Buick; she almost ran because she knew how upset Mrs. Donohue would be if she had to wait a moment more than necessary.

Hannah was half inside the car before she realized that the driver wasn't Mrs. Donohue at all.

"Hi," the driver said. "I'm Greg."

Nightfall

HANNAH BLUSHED CRIMSON AND FELT A WILD urge to scramble out of the car.

"Mrs. Donohue's grandson," he added quickly.

All she could manage was "Hi."

"She sent me. The traffic gets to her." He looked at Hannah while she wrestled with the seat belt, which had got stuck in the door. "You'll have to open the door again," Greg said.

Feeling really dumb, Hannah opened the door and pulled the belt in.

Greg waited until the door closed. The seat belt still seemed to be stuck, and Greg had to lean right across her and pull it free. She could smell his after-shave. Greg's arms were tanned, while Hannah still had what Melanie called her prison pallor.

"There," he said when Hannah was safely buckled. "That's

embarrassing; I put these seat belts in myself. Now let's face the famous Edgartown traffic."

Once Greg had the car in gear, he slipped his sunglasses on and maneuvered the Buick effortlessly into traffic.

Hannah leaned back in the seat, her purse on her lap. Despite the confusion, she had a clear picture of Greg. About eighteen, she guessed. He was tall, with an athletic build. He was dressed casually in dark blue shorts and a T-shirt a couple of sizes too big hanging loosely from strong shoulders. His hair had been bleached by the sun to the color of corn silk. He was certainly what Melanie would call a hunk.

Greg flicked the radio on and drove directly north, avoiding the center of town.

Hannah was furious at herself for acting like some preteen and embarrassed that Greg might know she was seeing a psychiatrist. Even now she was pretending to be looking at the scenery while sneaking one or two looks at him.

With an effort she said, "I'm Hannah." And then was mortified to hear how stupid it sounded.

He turned to her with a wide, pleasant grin and nodded. "I know."

Still unable to look directly at him, Hannah sat clutching her purse and feeling like a third grader on the first day of school. What would Melanie have said? "They are just like us, my dear—except where it matters."

Then, to her horror, she found herself beginning to laugh. She quickly turned the laughter into a fit of sneezing.

"You all right?" asked Greg.

"Yes. It was . . ."

"Allergies," he said knowingly. "Lots of off-islanders get them. Must be the sea air."

It took a few seconds for her to realize he wasn't serious. Then they both laughed, the tension broken.

Greg edged his way around a van only to be halted at a pedestrian crossing by a troop of boy scouts. "A hundred thousand people during the season, if you count day trippers," he commented. "And there's only one traffic light on the Vineyard."

They kept up a conversation of sorts, Greg doing most of the talking, until at last they were in Stewart's Lane, with its leafy canopy and thick carpet of wildflowers. "I want to take it easy here," Greg said, slowing down to a crawl. "I once met an off-islander coming the other way. I swerved into the ditch, and it cost thirty-five bucks to get towed out. He didn't even stop." Greg gave a humorless laugh.

"The off-islanders are not very popular, are they?" Hannah asked tentatively.

"Why should they be," he snapped, coloring. "They come over here and push us around—just because they're rich and used to getting what they want. My parents move to Boston during the season. Can't stand the crowds and the noise." He was frowning and gripping the wheel tightly. "And people like me are supposed to be grateful because we get a scholarship to college. Rich kids just buy their way in."

There was an embarrassed silence; Hannah felt a tightening in her chest. She was sorry she had spoken.

"They wouldn't want to be here in the winter though. Everything freezes; there's skating on Sweetened Water Pond; icy blasts from the Atlantic. The population drops to about ten thousand, and we're the coldest, sorriest people you ever saw. High-school kids in Menemsha have to be up at five to catch the school bus. It's pitch black."

He turned onto the long gravel drive. Hannah wondered if she'd be one of those sorry people. Would she be attending the high school in the fall? She didn't know a single kid on the island! How would she get to school? She couldn't imagine Mrs. Donohue driving her every morning. Worse still, suppose she herself had to drive the Buick?

"Do you work here every summer?" she asked, more because she felt she should say something than for the information.

"Sure. For Mrs. Chase, and I put in a few volunteer hours at the Marine Research Lab. I'm gonna start my freshman year in marine biology at U. Mass. in the fall." He became animated. "I wanted to start on sharks. No one knows how fast they grow, how long they live, how often they reproduce, or where they migrate to. I wanted to find out."

Hannah shuddered. "Haven't you seen *Jaws?*"

"Seen it! I was in the last one—two quick shots of the back of my head," said Greg, laughing as they pulled up by the luggage entrance. "Anyway, at U. Mass. they start you on shellfish. Around here the molluscs and crustacea are pretty important, though there seem to be fewer of them each year. The whole ecology of the island's overwhelmed by the off-islanders' pollution and the overcrowding."

"But it must be interesting working with animals or fish. It'd fascinate me," Hannah said. "I'd love to go miles below the ocean in one of those submarine things."

"A submersible?" He looked at her. "Me too. I'm the Jacques Piccard of the Vineyard set. Most of the kids think I'm crazy. They all want to be stockbrokers and lawyers."

"How boring."

Greg shifted into park, turning the engine off. "You're right, but people don't care about wildlife when it gets in their way. Did you know the Vineyard was the last place on earth to have a heath hen? The absolute last one. They're extinct now. Your aunt's different. She doesn't like unnecessary change. She appreciates living things. She's got the finest mountain laurel on the island."

Hannah opened her door, stood on the gravel, and looked around. "Where is it?" she asked curiously.

Greg had gotten out of the car and was leaning over the roof to talk to her. "In the conservatory. You know, in the west wing."

"I thought the west wing was shut up."

"Come on," said Greg, walking around and taking her lightly by the arm. She felt tiny ripples of excitement run up her spine.

"The touch of a good-looking young man, my children," Melanie proclaimed one night to the other students, "is a thing of beauty and a joy forever."

He guided her up the steps and once inside turned sharply to the left, and they descended half a dozen stairs. A set of French windows, with the glass painted white, opened to his touch.

Hannah gasped in astonishment. Everywhere she looked, there were flowers and shrubs. Beds of zinnias, daylilies, irises, carnations, and snapdragons were arranged in a formal design like a giant multicolored wheel. In the middle of the conservatory was a huge bush, covered with thousands of small white star-shaped flowers. The roof above them consisted of dozens of panes of glass in three great arches.

"It's about thirty feet long," remarked Greg. "Grandpops does all the work. It's called Walnut Tree Court, but the walnut died years ago, and Mr. Chase planted this mountain laurel. Grandpops keeps this up as a hobby. No one comes here these days. Come on."

41

Leading the way, he crossed the conservatory. "Downtown, on South Water Street, there's a huge pagoda tree. A Captain Milton brought it back from China in a flowerpot. Now take a look at this." He opened a set of heavy windowless doors. A long, dark passage greeted their eyes. She shivered; the air was icy.

"That's Long Walk, Hannah. Two hundred feet from here to the end. Up there"—he pointed to their right, though they could see nothing through the darkness—"is a set of double doors, and beyond them is your room."

"Long Walk is fairly new, isn't it?" asked Hannah.

"Sure, if you call a hundred fifty years new. The old buildings like the kitchens were built right on the site of an old Puritan farmhouse. The style of this house is 'anything goes.' Grandpops thinks it's haunted."

"Haunted?" exclaimed Hannah.

"Don't you know all old buildings are full of ghosts? I expect there's some old guy who carries his head around under his arm. Grandpops swears some Puritan maid glides around here late at night. She doesn't have a loose head, though."

"Oh, don't," said Hannah.

Greg laughed and stepped across Long Walk to the far wall. She could barely see him. The only illumination came from the conservatory behind them. She felt the urge to sneeze and tried unsuccessfully to stifle it.

"Dust," said Greg. "I'm gonna move one of the drapes."

A high triangle of light spilled onto the opposite wall. Now through the windows she could see the formal gardens behind the house and more of Long Walk to her left and right. It was just possible to make out several sets of red plush drapes and some of the red and gold motif of the paintwork stretching down Long Walk. Nearby a small statue sat on a tall round base. She could make out another one some twenty feet away. Then Greg let go of the drape.

"No one's been here for years," he said, leading the way back through the conservatory. "When a big storm is brewing, I get to close the shutters outside Long Walk." He grinned ruefully. "All fifty of them. I'll have to do them today, by the feel of things. Still, Mrs. Chase lets me have a clambake on her beach once a summer, so it's worth it."

They were back outside the luggage entrance. "I've got an idea," he said. "Tomorrow I'll get a couple of bicycles and show you some of this side of the island."

"You don't have to do that," she replied defensively, but as she spoke his gaze caught hers. Hannah felt her cheeks redden. What did he think of her? She was both nervous and exhilarated, and to cover her confusion she turned away and was embarrassed when the door wouldn't open. She gave it a hard push and turned to steal a last look at Greg. He was still watching her as she hurried inside.

On the table in the alcove was a letter addressed to her in a familiar flowery hand. She ran back to her room with it and almost tore the envelope apart in her eagerness to read its contents.

The Booby Hatch
Thursday?
Library (Cataloging,
the inner sanctum)

Dear H,

What's up? How come you haven't written to me? I guess you didn't get there yet. I'm going crazy, well I am crazy, but I'm going crazier. The two new kids are nerds. Depressives the pair of them.

One of them told me there was nothing wrong with her. It was ALL A PLOT. Oh boy, I guess we all heard that before!!!

I miss you and the crew, you guys were fun people; then you got cured.

Today Mrs. P. is threatening to do inventory. If she does ALL WILL BE REVEALED!!!

Miss Miscliewsky has flown the coop! Apparently that guy she was a heavy number with in the village was married! Oh scandal! When the word got out, she took off for Michigan or somewhere equally ghastly.

Under Virgo, your horoscope reads "Romantic developments speed up. Your fantasies can become realities. Beware of past events, they may catch up with you." Under Taurus, my dear, it says "Men in your life will become more generous." That wouldn't take much.

How's Grumps?

There's a new French teacher, and he's a MALE. He's got soulful eyes, and I just go *gaga*, my dear, when he talks that stuff.

"La plume de ma tante est sur la table" or is it *"le table?"* How can you have a male or female table? Is that why the French are supposed to have sex on their minds all the time?

I bought some Shine Free Coloribbons. Twelve kinky colors. I'm letting my tresses run wild. I look very French.

Are you going to write or what? Have you met any MALES? Oh God, I think I'll go madder.

Love ya always,

M

P.S.   Send me a picture of the male if there is one. I'll try to get one of Monsieur Desmoullins. Can you believe the name? Oh God!!
P.P.S.   STOP PRESS. WILBANKS SAYS I MAY BE GETTING OUTTA HERE SOON!!!

44

She had underlined the second postscript three times.

Hannah found a pad of writing paper and began a reply at once.

Stewart's Grove

Monday

Dear Melanie,

Is it true? Will you be getting out? Can you come and stay here? Oh God if only we can see each other again!

I have to warn you. This place is a bit weird. There's my great-aunt, Mrs. Chase, who almost never leaves the island, her housekeeper, Mrs. Donohue, who says things were better before the war, don't ask me which war, and her husband (she calls him Mr. Donohue) who sees ghosts! and grows beautiful flowers. My shrink, Dr. Marsh, is a woman and a lot stranger than Wilbanks, but nice.

Well the Donohues have a grandson called Greg. He's just graduated high school and will start college in the fall. He's got blue eyes and blond hair. Can you believe it? We spent a morning together, and we're going bike riding tomorrow. He's got to be the best-looking guy on the island.

Do you think this ride tomorrow is a date? Or is he just being kind?

He showed me around the old part of the house (the bit that's supposed to be haunted). It's shut off because my great-aunt can't afford to keep it up. I'm right next to it. Just down a short passage is a hall called Long Walk nearly a hundred yards long and a conservatory half the size of a football field. I was freezing in the hall, and it's eighty-five degrees outside.

Tell me more about the French teacher. I thought you dropped French.

How are you going to fix the library cards?
Grumps says hi. He misses you.

Love,
Hannah.

When she read the letter over, Hannah was far from pleased with it. There wasn't enough about herself in it. She wanted to add she felt fine, and she did. A year ago the thought of going to stay with someone she didn't know would have terrified her. She realized with a start she had said more to Greg than to any boy she had known in three years. When she first went to Reach Out, she could barely talk to a stranger.

For the time being the letter would have to do. She wrote out the familiar address on an envelope and found a book of stamps in her purse. As an experiment she left it on the hall table. She was sure it would be picked up and delivered by some process long ago perfected by Mrs. Donohue.

Hannah loved to read. She examined the books in McGlynn's room. Apparently the butler read only classic novels. There were a dozen by Dickens and several by Sir Walter Scott. She found *Cranford* by Mrs. Gaskell and a battered copy of *Middlemarch* with its cover torn. A price of 50 cents was written in pencil on the title page.

There was a copy of *Pride and Prejudice*, which Hannah had finished the day before she left Reach Out. Picking out the copy of Emily Brontë's *Wuthering Heights*, she lay on her bed and began to read.

The rest of the day passed quickly as she became more engrossed in her book. Meals with her aunt were merely an interruption; Mrs. Chase had little to say and didn't encourage conversation. Mrs. Donohue, besides being cook, was also server. At each course, Mrs. Chase uttered her standard words of praise, and Mrs. Donohue seemed content. At dinner all her aunt said was that it was certain to storm.

Mrs. Donohue nodded her agreement. "There'll be a blow all right. Fishermen been coming into harbor all afternoon. A lot of crab and lobster pots will be lost. I told Greg to close the shutters on Long Walk."

Hannah went back to her room as soon as she could. After reading for an hour or so she felt restless; she could sense the storm beginning to build. There was an almost constant rumbling in the distance over Vineyard Sound. She reread the passage in *Wuthering Heights* where Lockwood rose from his bed to break off a branch knocking against the window of his room.

"I must stop it, nevertheless!" I muttered, knocking my knuckles through the glass, and stretching an arm out to seize the importunate branch: instead of which, my fingers closed on the fingers of a little, ice-cold hand!

A sudden loud crash of thunder startled Hannah, who let out a scream, dropping the book.

"I'm spooking myself," she muttered, closing the book and putting it on the bedside table. She thought of going into the north wing but decided her aunt would not welcome her company. Anyway, what would they talk about?

She rummaged through her cassettes, but nothing appealed to her.

"Well, there's only one show to see," she said to Grumps,

pulling back the drapes and switching the light off. She knelt on the window seat, elbows on the broad sill. Above Vineyard Sound, the sky was barely visible. Then a great branch of lightning illuminated the formal garden and the cliff beyond.

There was a lull in the wind, then with a suddenness that startled her the thunder crashed all around Stewart's Grove.

Suddenly, great forks of lightning lit the night sky. Ragged black rain clouds fled across a purple backcloth.

When the lightning flared again, it was closer, much closer. In that brief but powerful illumination she thought there was someone standing near the rock garden under the great boughs of Stewart's Oak, a man with a broad black hat who seemed to be staring up at her.

Hannah's head jerked back; it was as if she were recoiling from a blow.

The rain was now streaming down, slashing against the windows in all its fury. Above the beach, beyond the cliffs, the storm came in across Vineyard Sound in awesome rolling thunderbolts, an eruption of ragged shards of white-hot light.

Hannah darted her head from side to side, hoping that with the next flash she would catch sight of whoever it was. It didn't look like Mr. Donohue, and anyway, he would have the sense to take shelter at a time like this.

Then there was a late burst of lightning, weaker and farther away. Hannah peered in the direction of the oak tree. No one was there.

She closed the drapes; they were thick and heavy, and the rings clacked as they ran along the rod. She shook her head;

her imagination was working overtime again. Worse, she was doing it to herself.

Following Melanie's advice, she took a shower and washed her hair. "Nothing like a shower to set things right," Melanie used to proclaim. "You can't feel crazy in the middle of shampooing your golden tresses."

Hannah was very tired; after all, it had been her first full day on the island. The bedside light had its own switch; she turned it off and snuggled into the sheets and lay listening to the last of the storm.

But she couldn't sleep. A lot of the confidence she had felt when she was writing to Melanie had disappeared. Facing Greg and spending a full day with him became a scary thing. What would they talk about? She played over in her mind their meeting and what he had said. Did he think she was a silly kid? Just how much did he know about her? Surely he must have a girl friend, one who would be going to college too. She would be seventeen, probably eighteen, and very sophisticated.

Several times she considered backing out. She could have a headache. Cramps. No, that would be the worst agony of all because then she'd never know what he thought.

Hannah was becoming drowsy at last. She yawned; for a time she was motionless, almost asleep. Then she thought she heard a sound beyond the door. She listened intently.

Nothing.

Nothing. Not the storm outside, not even the creaks that are always heard in old houses. Inhaling deeply, Hannah steadied her nerves. She was acting like a kid. Now she really was tired. Washed out.

Something cold touched her spine. Without seeming to

awaken, Hannah sat up. The room was utterly dark. The chill spread through her from toes to scalp. On the nape of her neck, the fine hair was charged with electricity.

Hannah drew a long, slow breath, trying to still the pounding of her heart.

And realized, with blinding certainty, she was not alone!

Gay Head

HANNAH SAT BOLT UPRIGHT, TRYING TO CATCH her breath. The room was very cold. Her throat was dry.

The chill remained. Around the edges of the door there was a faint glow in the darkness. The door rattled violently as if a great blast of wind had hammered against it. Then it swung open violently, slamming against the wall.

At first there had been nothing but a faint glow in the darkness. Slowly a figure began to form before her. It was like smoke curling in upon itself, eddying and flowing. Then beyond the end of the bed a face struggled to be born, its features still vaguely defined and insubstantial.

The face shimmered and slowly defined itself. It was that of a girl about her age; Hannah could pick out the face, pale yet pretty.

As if caught between two worlds and times, the vision pulsated, fading, then strengthening. In its most defined state,

51

Hannah could see a Puritan dress, a long black gown with a large white collar, a fitted long-sleeved jacket, and a white apron over the skirt.

Hannah turned her face away, closed her eyes for a second, then looked again. The pallid face had lost most of its features.

Yet Hannah could not have misunderstood the look of anguish. The mouth formed words and seemed to repeat the same phrases over and over, but no sound came from the pale lips.

The apparition turned and crossed toward the door; it did not glide as she had expected but walked slowly and purposefully. Hannah was not frightened; the ghostly figure did not appear threatening.

Then she heard the grandfather clock chime far away in the north wing. Two stately chimes—the vision faded, and the room became dark.

"This is all a dream," said Hannah sharply to herself. "No one believes in ghosts anymore." She hadn't been threatened, and she wasn't afraid.

"I've got to stop this," she said firmly to herself. "I'm acting like some dumb kid who's afraid of the dark and seeing ghosts." She could just imagine her aunt's reaction if she told her Stewart's Grove was haunted!

So Hannah lay back against the pillows, pulling the sheet and blanket closely around her, thankful for the quilt. Other sounds became audible. The wind had risen. In the distance, the surf pounded the beach; the tide was coming in.

How long she lay there she had no way of knowing. In the night her hearing was more acute. The grandfather clock in the north wing sounded the quarters regularly. She quickly learned the different lengths of its chiming.

She found herself thinking of her mother. They hadn't had enough time together. There had been too few occasions when Hannah had watched her in court defending clients. Or, in the evenings after supper, either playing the baby grand in the front room or walking with Hannah and her father down to the park "to clear the cobwebs from my brain," as she put it. Yet the thought of these times they had had together was comforting.

She remembered nothing more until she awoke the next morning. The drapes kept the light out, and for an instant she was disoriented. The sensation soon passed, and she felt along the cord of the bedside lamp until she found the switch.

"Thank goodness," she muttered as the light came on. It was a relief to be able to get up and start the day. Having found her slippers, Hannah crossed the room and pulled back the drapes. In the light outside, everything looked fresh and alive. The ocean was calm and as blue as a picture postcard; she could hear the surf only if she concentrated; occasional gulls rose above the cliff, borne on updrafts, sinking out of sight in their endless noisy quest for food.

Hannah looked for some way to open the windows but soon discovered they had been painted shut. Numerous coats of paint had sealed them as effectively as nails.

It was a perfect day for running. She hadn't taken part in athletics at school, but at Reach Out all physical activities were encouraged. Running gave her a chance to be alone for a time and to think. She suspected Dr. Wilbanks encouraged it in order to keep up a healthy appetite. Melanie had been astonished; she preferred to play tennis in a short dress, hoping some boys would see her.

As Hannah put her sweater on and left by the luggage entrance, she thought about how much she owed Melanie. It was their friendship that convinced Hannah of the foolishness of what she was doing to herself. *I still don't know how she did it*, she thought, running down the steps out onto the gravel drive. Gradually she had found herself eating a little more, and because she now had a friend, her sense of loss didn't seem so overwhelming. Six months before Hannah went to Reach Out, a girl had almost died of self-starvation. "She lost the will to live," Melanie had told Hannah. "But you're my best friend, and I need you." Then Melanie, tough, brassy Melanie, had burst into tears.

As Hannah had tried to comfort her, she had remembered that Melanie's illness was very serious—she had attempted suicide—and she could swing from one extreme mood to its opposite in an instant. As she held the sobbing Melanie, Hannah had promised she would do everything in her power to stop punishing herself. And she did, though it was harder than she ever had dreamed it could be. Without Melanie's constant support, she might well have failed.

All that was behind her, and Melanie, too, had made rapid improvement. Soon she would be going home. And then they would, they must, see each other again.

Running strongly, she passed under the huge branches of Stewart's Oak and followed the path to the gates that blocked off her aunt's beach. It took only a few seconds to climb over them and follow the dirt road to the ocean.

The tide was ebbing, leaving behind a boundary of seaweed and driftwood. A tiny crab scuttled sideways to the safety of the ocean.

For no particular reason, Hannah experienced a sudden feeling of exhilaration; she had these moods more often now. "You're getting well," Dr. Wilbanks had told her. "Welcome home."

Reaching the rocky headland at the end of the beach, she turned and ran back to the path that led up the cliff face to Stewart's Grove. The going was hard, but Hannah made it a point not to walk. The breath was being sucked into her lungs in great gasps, and she was exhaling just as rigorously.

Then she could see the top and minutes later stood on the cliff fifty feet above Vineyard Sound, gazing to the horizon where sky and sea met. The only sounds were those of waves retreating from the shore and gulls crying above her.

Back at Stewart's Grove she took a shower. The water tasted salty, and the force of it reminded her of how good it was to feel again, to be free of almost-constant depression. After months of hating and depriving her body, she could now accept it. At Reach Out when she had made her target weight, she'd told her delighted friend.

"We must cherish our bods," Melanie proclaimed, imitating the voice of old Mrs. Carroll, the school nurse. "Soon you must accept womanhood as a sacred trust." What made that all the more amusing was that Nurse Carroll always selected little-girl clothes for herself and still wore her hair in a ponytail.

Hannah was smiling to herself in her bedroom, pulling a brush through her hair, when the speaking tube sounded.

"Breakfast in ten minutes," said Mrs. Donohue faintly. "Mrs. Chase is always punctual."

Hannah had picked out the clothes she was going to wear, but now they looked all wrong. She tried on three pairs of shorts but didn't see how she could go to breakfast in them. So she selected a T-shirt and jeans. Despite the hair dryer and curler, her hair looked messy.

Her aunt was sitting by the fireplace, reading a newspaper; a cup of coffee was steaming beside her on an elegant side table. Mrs. Chase nodded, a great relief to Hannah, who wondered if she should peck her aunt on the cheek each morning. The answer was clearly no.

"There are a number of activities listed in the *Gazette*," she said, as Hannah took her seat. "Shakespeare's *A Midsummer Night's Dream* will be performed at the Tisbury Amphitheatre this Saturday; I shall certainly take you to that. I feel it is my duty to support any vestige of culture on the Vineyard. My husband was a patron of the arts. Last year the players did *Othello* in modern dress. I believe Emilia wore a leather miniskirt. Not to my taste. Mrs. Donohue said she didn't like plays written after the war."

Hannah looked up sharply from the piece of toast she was buttering. Had her aunt *really* made a joke? And at Mrs. Donohue's expense? Mrs. Chase's face revealed nothing.

"James Racquepau will lead a bird walk at Felix Neck," she continued. "I remember him when he first came to the island forty-odd years ago. Didn't know a tern from an osprey. My, how things change. Now he's an expert."

Hannah didn't think she should say anything, so she ate her toast.

"There is a film at the library called *Witch Board*. I know nothing about it; my taste runs to opera and ballet. You will notice there is no television in Stewart's Grove."

With a start Hannah realized her aunt was looking at her and that she was expected to say something. Hannah put the marmalade jar down. "I would like to see *A Midsummer Night's Dream*, Aunt Caroline." Then, as casually as possible, she added, "Mrs. Donohue's grandson said something about showing me the island." It sounded very lame.

"Gregory?"

"Yes." She felt suddenly she would die of embarrassment,

but Mrs. Chase had returned to the newspaper. "A very sensible young man. Not like most of his ilk." Without Hannah's noticing, Mrs. Chase looked at her from the corner of her eye. Seeing the look on her niece's face, she smiled to herself.

Greg was sitting on the top step by the luggage entrance with two Schwinn bicycles propped up on kickstands. On his back was a blue nylon Jetsport backpack. He was even better-looking than she remembered. His little half smile drove away the brief irritation she had felt at his self-assurance. He hadn't even *asked* her if she wanted to go. Still, she did, and why shouldn't she?

"I thought we'd take bicycles to Gay Head. It's about as far southwest as you can get on the island. Used to be a sizable Indian population living there."

She took the smaller bike; it was painted green, but rust had attacked the frame in places. When she pushed it forward, only the back brake worked well. Swinging her leg over the seat, Hannah circled the drive. "Okay," she announced.

At the school there had been many bicycles, so she had little difficulty keeping up with Greg's ten-speed. Together they pedaled along the drive, past the pine copse and the great lawn with its silent fountain. The lilacs at the end of the drive were heavy with scent; huge bumblebees lurched from one flower to the next, looking for pollen. One apparently flew at Greg by accident, and he stopped suddenly, almost falling. He flashed a quick embarrassed look at Hannah, who pretended she hadn't noticed.

"We'll take the North Road," he shouted over his shoulder when he had remounted, "but after a mile we take the South Road into West Tisbury."

Hannah was content to follow behind. The unpaved road

connecting the two main roads was heavy going, most of it uphill. She admired Greg's muscled and suntanned body again, so different from her own pallid one. His powerful legs drove the pedals effortlessly. Already Hannah was beginning to regret not having worn shorts. Jeans were too thick and heavy for cycling. It was already about eighty degrees, and it certainly wouldn't get any cooler until evening.

The island was far from flat; they climbed hills slowly and sped down the opposite sides. Sometimes they followed cart paths, their legs brushing against weeds and wildflowers. Hannah could name only one flower, Queen Anne's lace. Each plant had a flat-topped cluster of tiny five-petaled flowers supposedly resembling the queen's headdress. There was also a great deal of ragweed. She was familiar with that because Melanie suffered from hay fever and took great delight in chopping down the unfortunate weeds before they could flower.

Greg led the way up a rocky path, following a stone fence, until they reached a crude wooden gate. He called a halt, much to Hannah's relief. In the field was a small pond fed by a stream. Two sheep, hoofs deep in mud, were drinking contentedly. As Greg stood looking over the gate, a light wind stirred his hair. All at once he turned and said grudgingly to Hannah, "I didn't think you'd be able to keep up."

Hannah flushed. "Why not?"

"Most of the girls I know wouldn't ride a bike. Too undignified and too much work. They have to have at least a Spree. They'd prefer a chauffeured limo if they could get one out here." He sounded bitter again. Then he shook it off and turned to the pond. "Crocker Pond," he said, "and the stream is called Witch Brook."

"There were witches here?" she asked.

Greg shrugged. "No one seems to know. There are references to them on parts of the island, but witchcraft is always good for tourist trade. It's said several old women and a young girl were hanged, but no one knows for sure."

Hannah stopped fanning herself. "A Puritan girl?" she asked faintly.

"What else? I told you my grandfather saw ghosts. Puritans are the ones who believed in witches. Want a Coke?"

Greg reached into his backpack and took out two red cans of Coca-Cola. Snapping the tab back, he handed one to Hannah.

"Most people think of witches and Massachusetts as the same thing. There's a Witch Pond at Gay Head; it's supposed to be bottomless. A friend of mine, Chris Harland, went in with a rod and reel looking for yellow perch and came out with . . ."

He paused, burying his face in his hands.

"What?" asked Hannah anxiously.

"Came out with . . . with . . . the worst case of poison ivy I've ever seen."

"Oh, you," Hannah cried with relief, hitting him playfully on the arm. He doubled up, then staggered away, clutching his arm as if she had broken it. *He's got a great sense of humor,* she thought, *but surely he can't be interested in me; I've never had a boyfriend. And he's so sure of himself.*

Greg stowed the empty cans in his backpack. They remounted the bikes and, taking advantage of a slight downhill run, freewheeled all the way through West Tisbury.

They rode for a mile beyond the village before Greg turned off the highway onto a dirt road bordered on both sides by pastureland. "See those trees?" Greg said, coming to a halt, one foot on the ground, the other on a pedal. "They're beetlebungs."

They didn't look like much. They stood about twenty feet tall, with deeply scoured bark of a grayish color. The pointed leaves were dark olive-green, and there were small greenish flowers in clusters of three.

"Beetles eat them?" suggested Hannah.

Greg laughed. "They're famous. A beetle is a mallet; they were made from these trees and used to drive bungs into whale-oil barrels. 'Beetle,' 'bung,' get it?"

Hannah nodded. "I'm glad they don't hunt whales anymore. It was so cruel."

Greg nodded. "It was fair enough in Melville's time, I suppose; now it's just a slaughter. Come on."

In a hollow between some dunes they ate the lunch Greg had packed, then walked barefoot along the edge of a tidal pool. They were alone except for two men in visored caps and rubber hip boots patiently digging for clams on the far shore.

Greg was easy to talk to, and a good listener. But he and Hannah spoke only about generalities. She wanted to confide in him but was afraid he would think her behavior childish. After all, trying to starve yourself to death was real dumb. So was seeing ghosts, so she kept quiet about that. She did tell him about Dr. Marsh and her fondness for chewing gum. "I've heard good things about her," he said, but didn't ask any questions. For this Hannah was grateful.

Then they resumed their exploration. Greg led the way up a narrow side lane. They had to push their bikes through thickets of scrub oak. Finally they reached a clearing. "Here we are," he said. "My grandmother made me promise to collect berries." He handed her a bottle. "Be sure to stick to the path, and better take off your sneakers," he cautioned her, knotting the laces of his own together and hanging them around his neck. "It's going to get pretty wet soon."

Hannah took her Nikes off and slipped her crew socks into her pocket. Rolling up the legs of her jeans as high as possible, she followed Greg. The waterlogged ground squished beneath her feet and water bubbled up between her toes.

"Don't worry," said Greg, "no poison ivy here, and the pool is only four feet deep in the middle." He grinned a little self-consciously. "I went skinny-dipping here when I was ten."

Pulling aside part of the hedge, he continued. "The blueberries are gone, but there are plenty of dangleberries." He touched the flat blue berries hanging from long stems. "You collect those; I'll collect running blackberries."

Hannah set to work with a will. In no time at all she had filled her bottle and was screwing the lid on when she became aware of a sound above the murmur of the waterfall. It was a high-pitched chirping from inside a huckleberry bush. Peering into it and carefully moving the branches aside, she found a bird trapped inside, its wings fluttering wildly.

"Greg," Hannah called. "Look what I've found."

He waded over to the bush. "It's a tropical bird," he said in amazement. "What a beauty."

Hannah looked at it closely. It was smaller than a gull and had a vermilion bill, black markings, snowy-white wings, and most surprising of all, magnificent streaming white tail feathers.

"They're rare," Greg said. "Very rare. They used to be thought bad luck in olden times. Too flashy for the Puritans, I guess. A few of them get swept up here during hurricanes."

He peered at it, while its eyes followed his every move. "Now come on," he said softly; "let's see what the trouble is."

Hannah heard the branch snap, then more alarmed chirping.

Greg had a branch in his hand; the bird's leg had become caught in the fork of a twig. Greg gave the branch a swift shake, and the bird was loose, flapping indignantly into a pepperbush.

"He'll be okay," said Greg. "You should call the *Vineyard Gazette;* this is the earliest sighting ever."

They returned to their bikes and for the next two hours they took paths through tiny settlements, pine copses, and sand dunes.

Time passed quickly. "We're nearly there," Greg told her as they cycled Indian file across a narrow strip of land, dwarfed by giant cattails. Then the path wound up a hill, and at last they were close to the top of Gay Head. Below they could see cliffs rising in ragged ribbons of red, white, gray, yellow, and black clay. Behind them the lighthouse flashed its warning beacon, visible even in the afternoon sunlight.

"Over there," said Greg, pointing, "on a clear day you can just see the twin towers of the Newport, Rhode Island, bridge. Can you run? I'll race you to the lighthouse."

Dropping his bike, he took off up the rutted path toward the grassy area that surrounded the lighthouse. Hannah, caught by surprise, pursued him.

Greg had expected to win easily, but Hannah was much quicker than he anticipated. Even though he had sprung the idea of a race upon her and had the advantage of a surprise start, she was one step ahead of him as she touched the squat red-brick tower.

"Phew!" he gasped. "Grandpops said you went jogging, but I didn't know you were a track star."

As if it were the most natural thing in the world, he slid his arm around her, and Hannah was astonished at herself. Could she have even imagined a situation like this six months ago? A week ago? Melanie had lots of stories about being alone with boys, but the details were always sketchy. Now here she was, shy little Hannah Kincaid, being held by the best-looking guy on the island. Finally she had the courage to look up into his face; he was smiling. The light flashed again; she could trace its sweep across his face.

"This is my favorite view," he said quietly, as they both turned to stare out over the blue-green water.

"It's beautiful," agreed Hannah. "I can see now why the islanders don't want it spoiled by a crowd of visitors."

"I love the ocean," Greg continued, almost in a whisper. "Even though my cousin Rose drowned out there."

Hannah gasped; her eyes sought his face again.

"It was a long time ago. There were three of us kids, my two cousins and me. We were horsing around on the boat. Must have been told a hundred times to behave. Anyway, I pushed Rose, and she tripped on the deck and went over the side. She slipped right out of her life jacket and never came up. Her body was never found. It was my fault, though no one ever said so. She'd have been about your age now," he added sadly. "Her mother never got over it. They say she never smiled again."

She put her arms around him to comfort him. "I know. I feel the same way about my mother. I still can't believe she's gone."

"You must miss her a lot."

"Yes," Hannah said simply.

There was a long silence. Finally Greg said, "It's an awful cliché, but nothing can change what's happened. It mustn't be allowed to affect the future."

She snuggled close to him. He was right. Nothing could change what had happened. She felt another surge of exhilaration. "It's going to be all right, isn't it?"

He looked at her; his fingers traced the cleft in her chin. "Of course it is."

And somehow she knew it would be.

6
Long Walk

PERHAPS IT WAS THE EXCITEMENT, BUT HANNAH couldn't sleep. Greg hadn't kissed her, but he had said he wanted to spend time with her. She'd wanted to say something cool and sophisticated, but all she could think of was "sure." What a dummy he must think I am, she'd thought immediately afterward; but he'd just grinned, so it was all right after all.

In her mind she went over the whole day, picturing every line of his face and trying to visualize every look he'd given her. If only Melanie were here. She wanted someone to share her news, and a letter was a feeble way. Still, she would write first thing tomorrow.

Hannah tried everything from concentrating on the distant sound of the surf to reading a "Melanie Slumber Book." A slumber book was guaranteed to put the reader to sleep within twenty minutes. Melanie took great pride in selecting them. The prime criterion was that it had to have Mrs. Pascoe's enthusiastic endorsement. The books were always long—five hundred pages was considered merely adequate; it also helped if the author was famous.

"For you, my dear child," Melanie had said as Hannah finished her packing, "the dullest book I've ever heard of: *The Life of Samuel Johnson*. Borrowed just once in ten years, by—you guessed it—Mrs. Pascoe. Over fourteen hundred dreary pages in small print."

Hannah read for about five minutes before the yawns started; within ten she was barely able to keep her eyes open, so she closed the book, turned the bedside light off, and pulled the bedclothes up to her chin.

There was a certain pleasure in being able to choose when to turn her light out. At the school, the dormitory lights were on a timer. At precisely ten-thirty, out they went. The girls even began a countdown of the last twenty seconds. There had been many good times. Hannah smiled, thinking of the time Melanie had organized a kitchen raid. Four of them had slipped quietly down the back stairs at midnight and climbed back with enough food for ten. Their entire dorm held a midnight feast sitting around a fat bayberry-scented candle. Hannah didn't realize until later that she had eaten as much as everyone else and not given it a second thought. When everything had been eaten and two gallons of orange juice were only a memory, Melanie looked around and said, "Do we look crazy? Do we act crazy?"

"Yes" came the response. It was so loud, they abandoned the floor and flung themselves into bed. Melanie had to rush back, blow out the candle, and throw it into a closet.

Two minutes later Mrs. Pascoe, who had night duty, peered in with a flashlight.

Melanie, her voice slurred as if she were waking from a deep sleep, said, "Mrs. Pascoe, what's wrong? Is there a fire?"

"No, no, girl. Go back to sleep. I heard noises, that's all. What's that smell?"

"Burglars," said Melanie groggily. "We've got burglars."

"Go back to sleep, Melanie," hissed Mrs. Pascoe, her tone becoming urgent. "You'll wake everyone."

That was all the girls needed to hear. One by one, they stirred and began questioning the frustrated librarian about the burglars.

"There are no burglars," screamed Mrs. Pascoe frantically at the top of her voice. "Go back to sleep." And summoning what dignity she could, she spun on her heel and left, loudly slamming the door on a room convulsed with laughter.

Hannah's mood shifted; she was thinking of her own bedroom in Sylvania. It was the one place in the house she could call hers alone. She remembered the pale blue curtains, the watercolors on the wall, and the windows that let in the scent of flowers during the day and the coolness of a Midwest fall in the evening. Hannah had kept a porcelain Coldport Lady on the mantelpiece, and a row of costume dolls her father had collected for her on his travels.

Daddy had told her he was going to marry Gayle one

morning at breakfast before leaving for work. Hannah hadn't been able to say anything. Everything was happening too fast. Most of all she resented the look of happiness in his eyes. So she had just nodded dumbly.

After he left, her stomach was still churning. She had carried her plate to the sink and scraped off the bacon strips and the globs of yellow egg yolk.

Then she had gone upstairs, smashed the porcelain doll, and burned the dolls one by one in the fireplace. Then she had stopped eating. Two months later she had been in the hospital.

Putting such thoughts from her, Hannah lay in bed until a leaden feeling overtook her; it was not unfamiliar. The effect was similar to that of powerful sleeping pills. Her arms and legs settled heavily into the down-filled mattress.

How long she slept Hannah did not know, but at some point she became aware of noises outside the house. Another storm?

At first there was nothing but a deep moaning from far away beyond the cliffs. Then came isolated flashes of electricity in the sky; loud cracks of thunder resounded above Stewart's Grove. The storm's intensity grew; the rain became a downpour punctuated by the more staccato rapping of drops against her windowpanes.

Now fully awake, Hannah climbed out of bed and crossed to the window. The heavy drapes parted reluctantly. Outside the sky was full of dancing flashes of brilliant lightning; thunder followed, adding sound to light.

Hannah could see the long row of dark green shutters of Long Walk as sharp-edged cutouts. Beyond the cliffs, sea and sky were one and black.

A sudden flash, forked, with spectacular antlers, lit up the sky to the horizon and bathed her room in fragile silver light. For five full seconds every item was visible; then came the clap of a thunderbolt so close it seemed the house must have been struck.

It was not the house, however, that received the full force of the lightning, but Stewart's Oak. The gigantic tree that had stood for a century and a half was suddenly in flames. As Hannah watched transfixed, the huge trunk parted at the top and slowly, but with gathering momentum, divided down the middle. Constant flashes of lightning and the flames consuming the crown of the oak allowed Hannah to watch the death of the magnificent tree. Even with the windows closed and the raging of the storm, she heard the splitting of the trunk. Bark flew off to reveal livid white wood beneath, and with a crash Stewart's Oak collapsed amid a million tiny red sparks.

The thunder pealed again and again; rain fell in streaming torrents, but the flames consuming the remains of the oak continued to burn. She watched in awe and pity as the great tree died.

At last the storm's fury moved out to sea as if the oak had been its intended victim. Sadly Hannah closed the drapes.

She slept. What woke her was a sound, not loud, but one she had been braced for subconsciously. In an instant she was sitting up, muscles tense, heart pounding; the room was still dark. Flicking the switch proved fruitless. The bedside light did not work. She wondered if the storm had brought down utility lines.

Hannah was cold. So cold she could barely move. She sat still for ten minutes; then, outside the door, she heard the sound again. At first she had trouble identifying what it was. After a moment, Hannah heard it again; it was much closer. This time she knew. Someone was crying!

Somewhere in the blackness beyond her door. It was not the sobbing of a child. Hannah sat tensely, listening.

Silence.

I heard it, she told herself. I heard someone sobbing. "I do not believe in ghosts," she said out loud. "And a dream is not real."

I won't. I can't, Hannah thought. *I simply cannot open that door.*

And yet why not? Should she be afraid of someone, clearly female, who was crying? Could anyone in such distress be a threat?

Hannah was deathly cold. Getting out of bed, she slipped her robe and slippers on and reached for the doorknob. Hesitating, she had to brace herself. With a courage she barely knew she possessed, Hannah opened the door. Down the hall were the double doors and beyond, the terrible blackness of Long Walk.

As she stood with one hand on the doorjamb, listening, the only noises now were the occasional gusts of wind from the fading storm and the sharp intake of her own breath.

It wasn't a dream, she thought defiantly. *I heard someone sobbing.*

Then she heard it again—a moaning sound, half sob, half wail, and a long way off. It came from the void of Long Walk. She left the security of her room. Walked down the short hall and pushed the doors open. At the same instant her hands and face were stung by an icy blast. Hannah stood rigid, waiting, staring into the void.

The darkness was palpable; she believed that if she

reached out she would feel its resistance. Then she saw movement deep in the confines of Long Walk. At first there was nothing more than a spark of light as if someone had struck a match; the tiny wisp of light turned and twisted and grew as if waiting to be born. A luminescent fog writhed and entwined its fingers of light.

Hannah watched in fascination; the shape was slowly assuming a vague outline—it was becoming human!

It was a moment like that when a runner is about to begin a race. She moved forward one step. Now she was committed; one step and she could see nothing ahead but a bobbing, weaving glimmer of light. . . .

Behind her, the doors swung shut; the sudden draft startled her. She took a dozen hesitant steps in the direction of the light. All around was a darkness so thick she felt entombed. Then a thought struck her: all she had to do was open one set of drapes, and the failing light of the storm or the moon would supply enough illumination for her to see what lay ahead or to guide her back to her room.

Feeling gingerly ahead, Hannah reached for the drapes. Her hands found nothing. Panic threatened to engulf her. "I am *not* afraid," she said firmly, though she had no sense of direction. "I am not afraid."

It took an eternity to find a solid object. She realized it was the paneled wall opposite the windows of Long Walk, because there were no drapes. Standing with her back firmly against the wood, Hannah placed her hands in front of her, then marched forward. Twelve paces and her right hand touched something cold. She froze and groped in the darkness.

Then with a scream she jumped back from the object. Her hands had felt a human face—cold and unyielding.

"Who are you?" she asked, her body trembling, a tight knot of fear in her stomach. "What do you want?"

There was no response.

Hannah's initial panic began to subside; she forced herself to take a deep breath and count slowly to ten. "Well?" she demanded.

There was no answer.

"I know you're there," she said, longing for just a pinprick of light to guide her back to her room.

Then filled with a sudden overwhelming terror, she ran from the silent watcher, blundered in the darkness, and felt herself strike something. There was a loud crash and the sound of something breaking.

Then she knew why the face was so unresponsive. It was carved from stone. Relief swept over her. She had knocked one of the statues over.

With renewed confidence, Hannah felt for the heavy drapes. Her first good yank at them produced a shower of dust. She began sneezing and coughing. The second pull parted the drapes, but the expected light did not appear. On the outside of the windows were the great wooden shutters. Long Walk remained as dark as a coal mine.

A low sob came out of the darkness.

Hannah thought, but couldn't be sure, there was a patch of light in the distance. Carefully, one step at a time, she began to move toward it.

She walked the way sighted people do in unfamiliar darkness: hands outstretched, feet testing the ground in front for fear it might unexpectedly fall away.

Hannah was surprised at herself and, despite her rapidly

beating heart, proud. A month ago, perhaps a week ago, she would have collapsed in tears, or run back in terror, but now, impelled by something stronger than fear, she worked her way steadily down Long Walk.

The pattern of light was growing smaller, as if the darkness were erasing its edges. She had to strain to hear the distant pounding of the surf; no other sound intruded.

Quickening her pace, she banged into another pedestal. The bust rocked back and forth, but she was able to grab it and lower it safely to the ground. She used the statues to orient herself, but her progress after the ghostly figure was little more than a crawl. She tried to gauge the distance she had come. Long Walk itself was over two hundred feet. The Walnut Tree Court was thirty. If the pedestals and their busts were twenty feet apart, how many had she passed?

What if I've gotten turned around? she wondered. Pulling her robe closer around her, for she was still unnaturally cold, Hannah began feeling for the next bust.

She had counted eight pedestals when she became aware of a glimmer of light coming from the opposite side of Long Walk. She could just make out an archway flanked by two chairs. The light came from beyond. Carefully Hannah made her way across Long Walk and stepped under the arch. An instant later, she felt herself falling down three or four cold stone steps.

Hannah was dazed but not hurt and got to her feet when the apparition materialized scarcely ten feet away down the passage.

"Who are you?" Hannah called out loudly, trying to keep the fear from her voice.

She scarcely expected to receive an answer. However,

for the first time, she could clearly discern the outline of the Puritan girl she had seen the preceding night. She wore the same black outfit, its somber tone relieved by the pallid face and white collar.

The figure stopped and beckoned to her, turning away and traveling slowly. The cold flagstones froze Hannah's feet through the thin slippers.

The girl disappeared through an archway to her right. Hannah followed without thinking.

"Who are you?" Hannah asked, more quietly this time, when she caught up.

Silence. After a few seconds, the girl turned away and began moving swiftly along the passage.

Hannah hurried after her, quickly enough to see the figure turn into another side passage.

"What do you want?" Hannah asked. There was no answer, only the echo of her voice in the empty hall.

A feeble light spilled across the end of the passage. Warm air banished the cold. Around her were shelves covered in dust. A left turn brought her to a door, swinging open. She could make out the word *bakehouse* carved into it. Light shone feebly through a skylight high above. There was no sign of the ghostly figure.

Looking around, her eyes adjusting, Hannah noticed the high ceiling, with a dozen rusty meat hooks hanging down, and a great iron fireplace, with deep ovens for baking bread. Two long, dusty tables took up most of the space. Empty shelves and cupboards had once held pots, pans, and cooking utensils.

She felt very tired. It was nearly dawn. Through the skylight, Hannah saw the reddening of the sky and the last straggles of storm clouds.

It took only a few minutes of trial and error to find a door leading to the outside. The house key was safely tucked away in the stone vase beside the luggage entrance, and Hannah was soon back in her bed without anyone being any the wiser.

Clambake

SURPRISINGLY, HANNAH FELT RESTED THE NEXT morning despite her visit to the west wing, and before jogging she went out to look at the remains of Stewart's Oak. It was sad to see how little of the tree remained. A giant crater had been formed where the roots had been wrenched from the ground as the tree fell. All the foliage and smaller branches had burned away.

"Terrible shame, isn't it," a voice said behind her.

Hannah jumped. "Oh, Mr. Donohue. You startled me. I didn't hear you."

"Sorry. People do say I come and go like a ghost." He was carrying a power saw.

For a moment they looked at each other. Hannah longed to confide in him about the events of the night before, but she lost her nerve. *He'll just think I'm dumb,* she thought.

"Last of the great oaks," he said softly.

"I saw it from my window," she said. "One minute it was there, the next it was burning."

"Well, they say nothing lasts forever, Miss Hannah, but I loved this old tree. Something solid about an oak. I'll cut the roots first, then try the trunk. It'll be like cutting iron, I reckon. I'll be sharpening this saw a few times." As he turned away, she saw the great sadness in his face.

"Got to run," she said, wanting to get away. There didn't seem to be anything else to say.

"You have a good run, Miss Hannah," he said, over his shoulder. Seconds later Hannah heard the roar of the power saw followed by the protesting sound of metal against wood.

Hannah did not jog on the beach, choosing instead to go north of Mrs. Chase's property. Once she was among the pine trees it was difficult to find her bearings. She was barely able to find her way back, shower, and change and eat a light breakfast before Mrs. Donohue brought the Buick to the luggage entrance.

Hannah settled in beside the housekeeper, who had on a straw bonnet in preparation for the hot day she had predicted. Hannah, determined to learn from her previous mistakes, wore yellow drawstring shorts with a matching tank top and her sandals. The fabric was cool and comfortable, ideal for threatened heat.

Little was said until Hannah commented on the storm.

"Pouf!" exclaimed Mrs. Donohue. "That was nothing, girl; you should be here when we get a three-day no'theaster, then you can talk."

Across the island, the signs of the storm's passage could be clearly seen in broken fences and missing roof tiles.

"Was Mrs. Chase upset about Stewart's Oak?" asked Hannah as they joined South Gate Lane.

"Didn't please her."

"Mr. Donohue was cutting it up."

The housekeeper sniffed and quickly slowed down. Rain had washed out a large section of pavement; there was a six-foot drop-off. "He was cutting the roots. Wait till he gets to the trunk. He won't cut that up so easily," she said darkly, skirting the edge of the hole.

At Old Mill Pond they were directed south by a sheriff's deputy and rejoined the road by the airport. Nothing was landing or taking off, and they saw two light planes lying flat on their backs, wheels to the sky.

"Wouldn't get me in one of those things," said Mrs. Donohue predictably. "Weren't meant to fly. Anyone can see that."

After that nothing was said until Mrs. Donohue pulled the Buick into the high-school parking lot.

"Can't face the traffic," said Mrs. Donohue in her usual abrupt manner. "And I'm not running a taxi service. You can take the trolley to the kite store, then walk. I'll pick you up about one o'clock here."

The trolley did not run on tracks; it was a bus with its sides removed to allow the riders to see the sights and to allow the air to circulate. Hannah paid her dollar fifty and took the only seat, right at the back.

Since the crowds were as large as ever and as unwilling to move for the bus as for any other vehicles, the ride was leisurely. Hannah began to think walking would have been quicker. The driver good-naturedly honked at the visitors who were wandering along quite aimlessly as if unsure what their role should be. They reluctantly parted to let the trolley through, then closed ranks behind it.

Hannah knew the kite store was on the corner of North Winter Street. She saw it at once. There was enough breeze from the harbor to stir up a riot of color outside the store as long-tailed dragons, windsocks, and rainbow streamers fluttered and twisted from the porch supports. A large sign promised a kite festival.

Dr. Marsh's cat, Sigmund, eyed Hannah lazily from the birdbath as she passed, using only one eye and saving his strength for the bird that would never come. He allowed her to rub him behind the ears.

As Hannah opened the door, a voice called, "Come out on the balcony."

Dr. Marsh had on a striped cotton skirt and a red shirt. She wore silver earrings and no lipstick. "Sit here," she said, patting the leather armchair next to her. "Let me buy you a Coke."

There was an old-fashioned Coke machine against the back wall; at one time, Hannah noted, Cokes had cost a nickel. She heard the sound of a coin falling and a bottle sliding down a chute.

"I bought this thing at a garage sale," the psychiatrist added, popping the top off and handing the bottle to Hannah. "Ten filled bottles left. Even these old-style bottles are worth money. Once I had the machine, I sold the garage to some-one else." She paused. "It's a joke. Get it—garage sale—?"

Hannah smiled and sipped her soda; it was ice cold.

"How've you been?"

"Fine."

"No weepiness, sadness, unhappiness, boredom, withdrawal, physical complaints? No pushing the scrambled eggs to the edge of the plate? No yucky egg yolk down the disposal?"

"No. Really."

Dr. Marsh sat back, crossing her legs and looking first at Hannah, then at the Coke. "My God. That stuff cures everything."

Hannah started to giggle, then laughter followed. Dr. Marsh bought herself a Coke. "Nine to go," she said. "Wonder if I can get them refilled. Now, Hannah, I want to read you something," she continued, taking a folder from beside her chair. Flicking through, she found a piece of paper, put on her glasses, and read. "It's all a game! No one really loves anyone. Unless you conform to everyone's stupid rules, they hate you. No one lets me be myself. If I wear the wrong clothes, earrings they don't like, they get mad, they say I'm crazy. It's all a bunch of . . ." She looked up. "Do you know who said that?"

Hannah shook her head. "She sounds crazy."

"You said it." Dr. Marsh replied, putting the paper back in its folder.

"I did?"

She nodded. "Two years ago."

Hannah shook her head in disbelief. "After Mommy died."

Dr. Marsh said nothing.

"After Dad married Gayle."

"Right."

"Oh."

The doctor read the hospital workup. "Withdrawn. Weight: ninety pounds. Eyes darkly shadowed, sunken. Hair lifeless. Depressed. IQ 110. Estimated daily food intake prior

80

to hospitalization: 600 calories. Blood sugar low. Chloride level below normal. Cardiac enzymes normal."

Hannah watched Dr. Marsh. She remembered her first therapist. He wrote everything down on a clipboard, all the time looking at her and never once glancing down to see whether the writing was going in a straight line. After a while all Hannah could think of was whether he would be able to read his notes. Dr. Marsh never wrote anything down.

"Why was I sick?" Hannah asked finally.

"You tell me." The doctor rose and sat on the rail of the balcony, the ocean behind.

"I guess so Dad would have to take care of me again."

"And?"

"And leave Gayle." Hannah drank her Coke, wondering if she should say anything about Greg. In the end she decided not to.

She gazed past the doctor to the ocean beyond. Tiny sailboats wove around each other and got in the way of the lobster fishermen.

"I had a dream last night," she blurted out suddenly. "It was so real. I thought I saw a ghost."

For an instant Hannah thought a look of profound disappointment passed over the doctor's face. If so, she recovered well. "Tell me about it."

"There's something in the house that doesn't want to be there; it's a girl about fifteen, dressed like a Puritan.

"You had this dream when?"

"I'm not sure it was a dream; it was so real. It happened last night."

"Have you had it before?"

"No. I was certain the sobbing and what I saw were real.

I was sure I followed the girl down Long Walk—do you know what Long Walk is?"

Dr. Marsh nodded, leaning forward in her chair.

"It was a . . . a sort of a light with enough shape some of the time to be seen. Mostly it was just faint light without any form."

"I see."

Dr. Marsh had become totally engrossed by Hannah's story. "How did you feel?"

Hannah thought carefully. "Well, I wasn't frightened. I knew she wouldn't hurt me. She wanted my help, to tell me something, but before she could, she disappeared. I felt *close* to her—almost as if I was her. Does that make any sense?"

The words came out with a rush, but her eyes met the doctor's and Hannah didn't flinch.

"Tell me about it from the beginning."

Taking a deep breath, Hannah carefully related all that took place from the first muffled sobs outside her bedroom door to the disappearance of the Puritan girl near the bakehouse.

The psychiatrist listened with the utmost attention. When Hannah had finished, she asked for clarifications on several points.

"Did the girl seem to recognize you?"

Hannah shook her head.

"Has anything like this happened before?"

"No . . . well . . . I've had some funny daydreams—I guess they were dreams."

"Tell me about them."

"On the first day here, in the car from Vineyard Haven, mist seemed to come up from the ocean and surround the car. I was tired, and I must have dozed off. The next thing I knew, I was dreaming about a witch being branded and hanged."

"Did you discuss this with anyone?"

"No. It was just a dream."

"And last night. You say you never had a dream that seemed so real."

"Never."

With lips pursed, Dr. Marsh hesitated, then said, "Describe the cold you felt."

"It was as if someone took the heat out of me."

"Not as if you walked into a cold place."

"Not at first. Later I thought it was cold in Long Walk."

There was another long silence; then Dr. Marsh said, "But you are experiencing threatening dreams—"

"I wasn't really afraid," Hannah broke in. "I felt the girl wanted me to do something, but I didn't know what."

"Why do you say that?"

"She was trying to say something, and it was very important to her. I could see that in her face. But I wasn't afraid."

"No, I don't think you were. If it had been me, I wouldn't have followed a ghost in the dead of night. But something's going on, and what I want to do is help you talk about how you think about yourself." She reached for a packet of gum and opened it. "If you can gain a sufficient insight, the depression and the dreams should disappear forever."

Hannah shuffled her feet on the worn carpet. "Sounds complicated."

"Not really. We all feel better after a good cry—at least I do. When we talk about things, bring them out into the open, we also feel better."

"But will I be able to talk about things? I mean, won't the memories be painful?"

"They might be, so I have a suggestion. Dr. Wilbanks suggested this, by the way. I'd like to hypnotize you."

Hannah sat back in astonishment. "Hypnotize me?"

"Yes. No one can force you to agree. If you do, I believe we can bring to the surface a great deal that lies buried. It is a technique that has been very useful in assisting people to remember things that made only a limited impression on their conscious mind." Dr. Marsh added, "Most of us appear to forget things, but we seldom do. They're all there if we knew how to get at them. Hypnotism should offer relief from hidden painful experiences."

Hannah was surprised and nervous. "What would I have to do?" she asked hesitantly. "I mean, if I agree."

"The first stage is to induce the trance. You can sit on the chair or lie on a sofa. Then you let yourself become completely passive. You accept things and ask no questions. You will focus on a bright object. Then I will put you in a trance; you will be awake and aware—but only of what I suggest to you."

"How do I go into the trance?"

"I ask you to look at an object, then I attempt to produce in your arm a feeling of heaviness until you cannot move it because it is so heavy."

Hannah got up and walked to the edge of the balcony and looked out over the harbor. "Will it stop the dreams?" she asked.

Dr. Marsh cleared her throat. "No guarantees, Hannah. Not in this game. Hypnosis is only an instrument; just as you repair broken bones under anesthesia, so I can treat emotional and psychological problems under hypnosis."

84

Hannah nodded. "If you think it will help."

"I believe it will. The hope is hypnosis will bring into focus thoughts and memories that are now hazy and confused. I'll try to go back into your past and uncover any deep underlying problem."

"But how can that help?"

Dr. Marsh shook her head. "It may not. Often, however, there is some deep psychological scar that is triggered by some tragedy. The technique is called regression. I have used it with some success."

"Oh," said Hannah, doubtfully.

"Let's meet again," Dr. Marsh said, consulting a small black-leather appointment book. "Lord, am I filled up. But I do think it's important that we investigate this ASAP. Let's see ... Sunday at ten is the only time I could see you. Okay?"

"Sure," Hannah replied, getting up. Dr. Marsh came to the door with her. Outside nothing had changed. Sigmund did bestir himself enough to stand on the birdbath and arch his great back. Then, with a lightness and grace that belied his size, he sprang to the grass and ran up to rub himself firmly against Hannah's leg.

"You've certainly made a hit with that cat. I've never known him take to anyone the way he does to you. Usually Sigmund just glowers at people," said Dr. Marsh. "Of course, it is feeding time. They have us so well trained, these animals. They understood Pavlov. This monster pretends to love me too, but only until he gets his Meow Mix." Scooping up the tabby, she turned back toward the house, saying over her shoulder, "See you Sunday."

Hannah looked back only once; Dr. Marsh had not reentered her house. Instead she stood on the top step, still staring after Hannah, Sigmund firmly in her grasp.

It was too hot to hurry, and anyway Hannah had only a vague idea of how she could kill the time. The shops looked inviting enough, but the crowds were a turnoff.

At least North Water Street was cool; giant elms and honey locusts filtered out the sun. There was something odd about the street, but she couldn't think what until she stopped and looked out to sea. The beautiful doors with their carved cornices were all at a bit of an angle to the street because they faced the harbor entrance and the lighthouse.

Perhaps because she was so preoccupied she didn't see Greg sitting on a whaling log near the city parking lot. He ran to catch up with her.

"Dollar for your thoughts," he said.

"I thought it was a penny," Hannah replied, hoping her voice didn't betray her emotions. He wore his familiar oversized T-shirt and shorts and sandals. The shirt proclaimed "Come Back to Jamaica."

"Not when they're that deep. You want a hamburger?"

Instinctively she started to say she wasn't hungry, but already he had taken her by the arm, the same electricity ran through her, and before she knew it they were in a small, very clean café. By the door was a huge ice-cream cone carved out of plywood.

"Maybe some ice cream."

"What flavor? They've got fifteen."

She chose pralines and cream. Greg had two large scoops of chocolate in a waffle cone.

They sat down at one of the little round tables whose tile tops showed witches on broomsticks. Tracing one with his finger, Greg said. "Wonder where they're flying?" he said.

"Probably to the sabbat," replied Hannah.

Greg looked up at her in surprise. "I didn't know you were an expert on witchcraft."

Hannah was as surprised as he. "It just came out," she replied. "Witches fly on broomsticks to meet with the devil at a sabbat. I guess I must have heard that somewhere and remembered it."

Shaking his head, Greg said with a grin, "Well, you're certainly something of a mystery."

"There's nothing mysterious about me," Hannah protested. "Nothing ever ..." She broke off. "That is until last night."

"The storm?"

"During the storm."

Greg was looking inquiringly at her. "Want to tell me about it?"

She told him all she could remember.

For several minutes Greg munched absentmindedly on his cone as if trying to digest Hannah's story of the ghostly visitor. Finally he said cautiously, "And what did the good shrink say?"

"She thinks it was a dream."

Greg thought about that before saying, "And you think it was too real?"

She nodded.

"Well, as I told you, Grandpops says the place is haunted. He would. The pair of them belong in a museum, don't you think?"

Hannah was startled. It seemed a very cruel thing to say.

Mrs. Donohue was a little strange, but kindly enough in her way, and her husband was as good-natured as anyone could be. She didn't want to make Greg mad, so she just muttered, "Maybe a bit odd at times."

"They won't stay at the big house, so we have to squash into a cottage outside Tisbury. There's a palace to live in, and they prefer a cottage. But I've never seen a ghost—with or without its head!"

Suddenly he let out a cry of alarm. "It's leaking."

The waffle cone was melting. Greg began sucking the ice cream through the hole as he reached for the napkin Hannah was handing to him. When he had successfully wrapped the bottom of the cone, he said, "Now I'm in the same mess as the Dutch boy who had to put his finger in the leaky dike." He laughed and began eating.

Hannah liked the way he laughed, the crinkle lines appearing and disappearing around the outer corners of his eyes, the firmness of his mouth, and the way his smile turned up more at one side than the other.

She was sure he must hear her heart pounding. A couple of times Hannah thought he looked at her as if she were something special but, of course, that was nonsense. A guy like Greg could have his pick.

All too soon he eased out from behind the table, taking her hand as if it were the most natural thing in the world. And it was just what Hannah wanted.

"We're invited to a clambake this evening," he announced.

Hannah let go of his hand; there was a familiar knot in her stomach. "Oh, I don't think—"

"And no excuses. Be ready at seven. You can't stay at Stewart's Grove every night. Anyway, I said you'd be there. And it's *my* clambake. There are people I want you to meet.

Lots of clams, no drink because Mrs. Chase disapproves, and a few lobster claws if we're lucky.

Again he laughed. Hannah hadn't felt this happy in a very long time. They met Mrs. Donohue at the school yard, and Hannah was still talking to him when they reached Stewart's Grove.

Greg had told Hannah to wear a swimsuit, so she did. However, she slipped a roomy red pullover over her shoulders in case it got cold later. From the bathroom, she took a towel.

She was at the luggage door promptly at seven, trying to appear casual, but her pulse was racing. A Jeep, with Greg at the wheel, sped up the drive. Before it had come to a complete halt, a large black dog with white feet bounded out of it and danced around her, barking furiously but joyfully.

"Wipeout! Get back in the Jeep," a male voice with a heavy New York accent shouted. "Or it's back to the pound for you." The dog didn't even look in his direction.

Greg jumped down. He was wearing cutoffs and a T-shirt with "Winner Vineyard Regatta—Sunfish" written across it in script. Grabbing the dog by the collar, he led it back to the Jeep, Hannah following.

"I'm Steve," said a young man about Greg's age. A pair of Bermuda shorts and a T-shirt with "New York Lacrosse Club" across its ample front added color to Steve, who resembled a teddy bear in designer sunglasses. A hat festooned with fishing lures completed the picture. He shook Hannah's hand vigorously.

"I'm Keri," said the blond in the backseat as Hannah got in beside her. She had a filter-tip cigarette between her fingers.

Hannah admired Keri's solid white polo shirt with pink striped collar and matching scalloped clam-digger pants. "You smoke?" Keri asked as the Jeep pulled into the drive.

"No." Hannah replied firmly. She regretted it immediately. Her father's new wife was always calling her "sensible" and "sweet." She hated the words. No one wanted to be known as sensible and sweet in high school. Those girls seldom got dates and everyone called them boring.

"Good for you," commented Steve, from the front. "It's a disgusting habit."

Keri leaned forward, tipped Steve's hat over his curly black hair, and pushed his glasses forward on his nose. Satisfied, she sat back and said to Hannah, "Boy, it's weird. What happened to all the old rituals and rebellious teenagers?"

"They got cancer," said Steve, taking care to keep his head out of reach.

"Oh pshaw!" said Keri, pronouncing every letter in the word but stubbing her cigarette out on the sole of her flip-flops. "You people are no fun, especially marine biologists and architects-to-be."

Somehow Hannah had been pleased to find Keri was cute rather than beautiful. Her straight brown hair was cut in bangs across her forehead, and the green eyes and turned-up nose gave Keri the air of a pixy. She still had braces on her teeth, whereas Hannah had finished with her retainer some weeks ago.

Wipeout was determined to lick Hannah's face, so Keri had to hold his collar.

"What kind of dog is he?" Hannah asked.

"Labrador retriever with a bit of Samoyed mixed in. The chewed ear was a present from some cat he tried to lick. Now lie down, you dumb beast."

Greg was following an overgrown trail to the beach. Soon they heard the waves crashing against the shore, and the tangy salt air filled their nostrils.

"Ah, breathe that ozone," said Steve as they bumped through the open gate, drawing up alongside a row of parked vehicles. "It's so healthy."

"A diet would do more good," whispered Keri to Hannah. "Bubba at one-ninety pounds."

"I heard that," said Steve. "And it's one-eighty."

"And I'm Abraham Lincoln."

Wipeout had bounded from the Jeep. Someone tossed a piece of driftwood into the surf, and with joyous barks the dog went paddling after it.

Hannah felt apprehension mingled with excitement as they climbed out of the Jeep. She wouldn't know a soul. They were probably all older and more sophisticated than she. Still, she was with Greg, and that was what mattered.

The beach was a hive of activity. Greg's guests were making a great deal of noise. A game of smash ball was in progress by the water's edge. At least half a dozen radios and tape players were blaring conflicting tunes.

Greg took a kettle from the back of the Jeep. With Steve following behind and carrying a basket, he led the three of them to the middle of the beach, where two young men were digging a shallow pit with short-handled spades.

One of them stopped, looked at Greg, and said with mock anger, "How come you arrive when all the work's done?"

"Joe, Frank, this is Hannah." Greg said. Then he added, "These guys are two of the most out-of-shape people you'll ever see. We'll take over."

Greg and Steve continued the digging.

"Ah," Keri muttered with a sigh. "I suppose we get to

collect the stones. That's the real work." She turned and faced the diggers. "Anyone can dig, but finding a few thousand stones, that's hard."

The rocks were used to line the pit, and Hannah soon saw what Keri meant. A dozen people were gathering driftwood and a similar number were collecting small rocks and throwing them into wooden and cardboard boxes. When these were filled they were dumped next to the pit. Hannah got on her knees to help.

She wasn't sure why, but something made her look up. A girl with long black hair that reached her waist was glaring down at her. She had the body Hannah dreamed of having, the perfect waist, and a well-developed bustline. She was carrying a terry-cloth beach robe and was wearing a cobalt-blue tiny bikini with a twist top that showed off every curve and emphasized long and slim legs.

The girl drew her hands through her long black hair, pulling it away from her face, which was twisted into a look of utter hatred.

Hannah felt her breath quicken and a cold sweat break out. A strange fear seemed to steal over her. She could not look away. The girl's eyes held hers prisoner; they seemed to bore into her head. Then she was gone.

Hannah fell to the sand; a sudden cramp had seized her left leg. She forgot everything else as she tried to straighten it. Gritting her teeth, she slowly extended her leg and foot, but the pain was excruciating.

Keri looked at her in astonishment. "What is it?"

"A cramp," she gasped, "in my leg." Then just as suddenly as it had begun the pain left her. The girl in the bathing suit had gone and was talking to one of the lifeguards.

Keri followed Hannah's gaze.

"Uh-uh!" said Keri. "That vision was none other than Miss Barbara Bonstelle-Whitely of the Back Bay Bonstelle-Whitelys. Commonwealth Avenue, no less. Last year she and Greg were very close. Then he found out she was also dating a guy in Boston and another one from Mount Holyoke. Boy, was that a scene. I thought he was going to hit her. He doesn't think much of the rich kids, and that didn't help."

"I know. What about you and Steve?"

"We go back to junior high, and Steve never talks about money. My dad owns a pet store on Long Island."

"A pet store!" Hannah repeated, in astonishment.

"Why not?" Keri shook her robe; sand fell from it. "Of course, it's no ordinary pet store."

They both giggled. "How long have you dated?" asked Hannah. "I mean, seriously."

"Two summers. The rumor is we're a strange match, but I like smart guys with ambition. He does tend to see conspiracies where no one else does, though—and I'm going to have to put him on a diet."

Both of them laughed again.

"And I'd much rather have you around than Miss B-B-W. I couldn't stand her with 'Daddy's yacht this' and 'Daddy's money that.' She comes to the Vineyard just to say how boring it is."

"She's very pretty."

"If you like gorgeous brunettes with sensuous lips, sapphire blue eyes, and high cheekbones. She's done some modeling too. That was when she dropped the Barbara and started calling herself Arielle. Even Steve, whose father could buy the entire Bonstelle-Whitely family, drooled over her. But listen." She held Hannah by the hand. "It's not looks that count. It's what you feel about yourself that matters. Guys only care about looks until they know better. Now let's lift."

Struggling, and almost falling in the fine sand, they carried their cardboard box toward the fire. "God," said Keri when she had caught her breath. "This is hard work."

Greg took their stones and arranged them around the edge of the pit. "Hannah, do you want to come to the fireworks?"

"Of course she does," Keri answered. "You do, don't you?"

"I don't know anything about them," Hannah confessed.

"It's supposed to be July Fourth," Steve said. "But the town fathers found they could have their cake and eat it. We have a Fourth of July parade—which you just missed—and on Saturday next, when it isn't July Fourth, we get fireworks."

"It's fun," Keri said, squeezing Hannah's hand. "Don't listen to this cynic."

"I'd like to go." Hannah shot a nervous sideways glance at Greg, relieved to see that he was smiling.

"I get to use our boat," Steve said. "That's the best part of the deal."

The wood ash was scraped from the stones and a layer of rockweed piled on them. There was a great cloud of smoke and a hissing as the wet seaweed damped the fire down. A strong salt smell arose.

Greg and Steve placed a layer of chicken wire onto the bed of stones and covered it with more seaweed. Then everyone helped spread the clams and added several dozen ears of corn.

The last stage was to drag a sail onto the pit. For one hour they had nothing to do but wait. There was dancing on the beach and a great deal of swimming and surfing. Finally, with great ceremony, the canvas was removed and the food divided up and the fire fanned into flame again.

Eating the shellfish was a problem. Hannah dropped her first two clams into the sand. She was sure she heard Arielle laugh and say, "I don't know where Greg finds these people."

"Ignore her," Keri said, in a loud stage whisper. "She only eats mountain goat and honey."

Arielle ignored Keri; instead she shot Hannah another look of pure hatred. "You don't belong here," she hissed.

"I'm here anyway," Hannah snapped back.

Arielle seemed taken aback. Trying to turn quickly on her heel, she stumbled in the sand. Two or three people laughed. Blushing scarlet, Arielle got to her feet and hurried away, got into a Jaguar XJS with one of the lifeguards, and drove off in a hail of sand and pebbles.

Hannah felt suddenly depressed. Arielle looked as if she'd stepped out of a fashion magazine. *How could Greg be interested in anyone as unglamorous as me?* she thought miserably.

Keri didn't seem a bit put out. "The girl hates your guts," she said cheerfully. "But who cares? Do you care? I don't; she's just jealous. Now Greg has someone whose IQ is in three digits, and who doesn't go on about 'Daddy's this' and 'Daddy's that.' B-B-W wants to waltz back into his life. No one invited her here. Of course, she would leave before the clean-up starts. Good riddance," she added. "I hope her hair falls out, the witch."

Everyone helped fill a dozen Glad trash bags and load them into a van. Greg and several of the boys were shoveling sand onto the fire. When its last flame flickered out, there was no need to light the Coleman lamps; the moon was shining brightly. Now it was time to leave. Most of the party-goers left in couples, the boys with their arms around the girls. Some were planning to walk along the beaches all the way to Edgartown, which would be somewhat easier as the tide turned and began its retreat. Buoys clanged in the distance.

Hannah rode up front on the way home. Sitting beside Greg made her feel important and a little possessive, because her date—and he *was* her date—was the driver. Greg parked the Jeep facing away from the luggage entrance. And he put his arm around her as they walked up the steps. By the door he took her in his arms, pulling her close. "See you at the fireworks, Hannah," he whispered.

But he didn't leave. He kept his arms around her. They were silent, each enjoying the nearness of the other. Hannah lifted her face, and slowly, gently, he pressed his lips against hers.

She'd half expected to be kissed, but when it happened Hannah was still caught off guard and had to close her eyes quickly. Greg's kiss was tentative at first, as if he wasn't sure whether she'd pull away. But she responded eagerly, not knowing until then how soft a young man's lips could be.

"You've got the softest hair," he whispered to her, gently stroking it. "I wanted to kiss you at Gay Head."

Then they kissed again. She closed her eyes and wished this moment could last forever. All too soon, they heard several light honks on the Jeep's horn. "Got to get back to Edgartown," Steve called out. There was the sound of a thump, followed by a puzzled, "Why did you elbow me, Keri?"

Greg sighed and gently kissed Hannah again before walking back to the Jeep and swinging himself into the driver's seat. Hannah stayed on the steps waving until the Jeep had passed out of sight beyond the gates.

When Hannah turned to her bed, all her good resolutions of taking a shower and washing the salt out of her hair were quickly abandoned. She slid gratefully between the sheets, slipping from wakefulness to sleep, and from reality into dream—and from dream into nightmare!

A Distant Light

8

IT DID NOT BEGIN IMMEDIATELY. FOR TWO HOURS,
Hannah slept, but as the grandfather clock struck midnight,
the dream that lay below her conscious state uncoiled itself.

It was night. The clouds breast-stroked across the disk of
the moon. Hannah was running after Melanie; they were in
a forest. The leaves of the trees met above her like the vault
of a church roof. Moon and stars penetrated only fleetingly.
They were on a broad, leaf-strewn path about fifty yards
apart. Melanie had on a long, white, flowing robe. Around
her neck and extending behind was a long, narrow, red scarf.
There was no sound.

The wood became darker, the night sky was invisible,
and the path began to narrow and twist around the trunks
of giant trees. The gnarled branches above seemed to have a
life of their own, arms of ill-shaped monsters lying in wait
above.

A surge of fear shot through Hannah, for she abruptly sensed that Melanie was in danger. "Melanie, no!" she cried silently as the outline of her friend swiftly fled deeper into the wood's dark embrace.

Melanie had vanished; in desperation Hannah peered around the trunks and ran from one clearing to another.

Finally she stood under the outspread limbs of a huge oak. Peering fearfully upward, Hannah saw a single bright-red thread. It was drawn as taut as a bowstring, as if some great weight hung heavily upon it.

The pain began in her abdomen, spreading rapidly to every organ in her body. Her lungs were one solid agony. There was no room for air; the passage was almost closed. Only great racking breaths would force air through it. A great lump blocked her throat; Hannah's hands instinctively grasped her neck. The air was sucked into her lungs with a loud, painful rasping sound.

Someone was screaming, a long way off. At first very unevenly, then with a great tearing feeling, she began to sob.

She lay there trembling until the tears subsided, until the constriction in her throat vanished. Until she realized it was she who had been screaming, with no one to hear her. When, at last, she looked around the room, everything was as it should be. Most importantly, feeling had returned to her limbs. She could move her arms and legs. She had come through. With an effort, Hannah reached out and flicked the bedside lamp on; the bulb glowed feebly. The familiar objects came into being around her—the table, the drapes, and the canopy above her bed.

Hannah was cold, ice cold, and shivering violently. Getting out of bed, she went to her wardrobe and put on a sweater and a pair of heavy running socks. In the mirror the reflection showed a slightly comical figure. As she ran her fingers through the tousled hair, a sudden chill wind, increasing to an icy blast, enveloped her, stinging her hands and face. The bedside light flickered, dimmed, flickered again, and then almost disappeared. Only a faint red glow surrounded the filament. The room filled with shadows.

A gray, leering face with a pale light of its own was forming in the mirror, and a luminous mist swirled violently by the door. Hannah stepped back, all her senses taut and strained. The eyes were fixed upon her, malicious and cruel. "You don't belong here," said a low, threatening voice. "Get back to your own time, and leave the witch to me." Then the figure faded, but not before she had a brief impression of a tall hat and black cloak.

And then without knowing how she got there, Hannah found herself looking into the blackness of Long Walk, a void disappearing into inky nothingness. There was an oppressive, brooding silence.

A shiver went through her.

She stood fearful and hesitating, peering into the gloom. There was no sound. She bent forward, eyes straining into the darkness, and then she saw it. Way in the distance, barely visible, was a tiny pinprick of light.

It was moving. Drawn to it, Hannah stepped into the void, eyes fixed. She did not feel carefully with her feet to see if the surface were level but simply launched herself forward, using the light as a beacon.

Hannah had scarcely covered half the distance when the light moved unexpectedly to the left and was gone. Now she had no beacon to guide her. She dared not continue as she had; instead, advancing cautiously, she tested the way with her foot, holding her hands up to protect her face.

She found the wall and the statues just as she remembered them. She *had* been there before!

The initial panic at being abruptly plunged into darkness began to subside. And steadying herself against the wall Hannah began to work her way down the hall.

"Is anyone there?" she called out. But her throat was dry, and the words came out no stronger than a whisper.

How silent it was. Except for the sound of her shuffling feet, Long Walk was absolutely still. "Who's there?" she demanded, this time more loudly. There was no response; she hadn't really expected one. And what if there had been one?

Moving as if in a trance, she edged her way down Long Walk. Somewhere ahead was the archway and the narrow passageway leading to the old kitchens.

She was groping along when it seemed something touched her face. Drawing back sharply, she put her hands out again and felt carefully side to side. She brushed against something fine and sticky. Shuddering, she quickly withdrew her hand and stepped back, but as she did so her ankle turned, and she fell.

Hannah dragged herself into a sitting position. "It's not going to defeat me," she said quietly but with determination. "Even if I have to crawl on my hands and knees until I reach the end of Long Walk." Her hand brushed against something hard and solid. She traced it eagerly with both hands. It was ...

"The chair," she breathed. "I've found one of the chairs."

She knew the doorway must be to the left or right of the

chair. Probably to the right. It was. The doors had been closed. Soon she had a brass knob in her hand; it made a little comforting rattle as it turned. Hannah pushed the door slightly open and listened. In the distance she thought she heard the sound of footsteps. Pausing, she took a deep breath and thrust the door wide open.

"Is anybody there?" Her words, immediately distorted by the shape of the passage and its stone walls, came bouncing back, incoherent and discordant.

In the passageway some light penetrated the gloom. Hannah stepped down and moved more confidently into the old part of the house.

Then there was a rustling sound, too definite to be dismissed as imaginary. An awful thought gripped her; she hadn't thought of it before. Suppose there were rats down here?

"Hello!" she said tentatively. "Is anybody there?"

This time she knew there were footsteps; they were unmistakable and approaching. She pressed herself against the wall, hoping against hope that she was mistaken.

A feeble light was shining from the end of one of the passageways; it was coming toward her.

Then Hannah lost her nerve. A wave of panic swept through her. Turning, she tried to flee but momentarily lost her footing. Abandoning herself to her fears, she ran desperately back in the direction of Long Walk. At once she realized she was lost. One stone wall looked like any other. She recognized nothing. One thing was clear; somehow she was going deeper into the recesses of the old wing, and not in the direction she wanted.

The ground gave way. For a fleeting irrational moment, Hannah thought she had found the steps back to Long Walk.

But they went down, not up. And there were more than two. Completely panicked, Hannah whirled around and ran back up the steps, pausing only briefly to listen, hearing only her labored breathing and the echo of what she prayed were her own footsteps. A door blocked her way. It was locked! Futilely, she pounded on it with her fists.

When a hand gripped Hannah's shoulder, the blood ran ice cold in her veins, and she let out a scream of pure terror, not daring to turn around and face whatever it was that gripped her. A beam of light caught the side of her face. Slowly she turned toward it.

"Hannah, is that you?" a voice asked from behind the light.

Almost too afraid to hope, Hannah replied shakily. "Who is it?"

"It's me. Greg." Strong arms folded around her trembling body.

"Greg! Oh, Greg, is it really you?" she sobbed. Her voice was high and sharp. It was all she could do to keep her knees from buckling as the tension drained from her in one sudden rush. "Greg. What are you doing down here?"

"I'm sorry," he whispered. "I didn't mean to scare you."

She lifted her head. "Scare? You terrified me."

Hannah felt him brush her hair away; his lips found hers. "I'm sorry," he said again.

"You look a rare sight," he said several minutes later as he shone the light on her. "Do you always wear a sweater to bed?"

"Don't you feel the cold?" she asked.

"Seems fine to me. Pleasantly cool, in fact."

"That's funny," Hannah replied. "It does feel warm now. Just a minute ago, I was freezing."

"I just came here to check out your story," Greg continued. "So I waited till everybody was safely asleep, or so I thought, and here I am. Of course"—he laughed—"you scared me a bit."

"Not as much as you did me. Why did you close the door to the passageway?"

"Dunno. It seemed tidier."

"It also cut off the light."

"Sorrrry!"

"You ought to be," Hannah said. "Now I know what a mole feels like."

He stood back, shining the flashlight about him. "If you don't mind, Madam, I would like to see the bakehouse. Once we do that, we can leave by another door. I know the way."

Hannah took the hand he offered her, and they quickly found the bakehouse door. Nothing had changed. Greg shone his flashlight at the giant fireplace.

"They probably roasted whole oxen in that," Greg remarked. "It's sure big enough."

Greg found a piece of half-burned wood in the fireplace, and used it to tap the walls. He looked up the chimney. "No light, but probably raccoons have nested there." He turned to Hannah. "Or bats."

"Ugh. Let's get out of here," said Hannah. "Twice is enough to last a lifetime."

"Only once," said Greg, pitching the wood back into the fireplace. "You must have dreamed the first time."

"Why do you say that?"

"For one thing, you left no footprints in some pretty thick dust. And all the busts are as forbidding as ever, and all in one piece."

Slowly Hannah followed him through the bakehouse door. "But it was so real," she said, shaking her head in disbelief.

"Magic," said Greg, ruffling her hair with his hand. "Any witches in your family?" And with a laugh he was gone, leaving Hannah to hurry after him.

9
Man of War

EARLY NEXT MORNING HANNAH WOKE TO THE distant sound of the grandfather clock striking six. Each chime hung lightly on the air until its successor drowned it. Knowing she would not go back to sleep, she put on her jogging outfit.

There was electricity in the air, and the sky was steadily darkening with torn, ragged clouds.

Hannah followed the cliff path north, the ocean on her left. A few gulls inspected her curiously from a distance before returning to the Sound. Once she frightened a rabbit that ran ahead of her before vanishing into the beach grass. At first she felt the effort of running, the breath being forced up from her lungs, the muscles tightening in her legs, and the pressure on her feet and ankles.

Then she was in her rhythm, all distractions forgotten. Her

whole body was working in harmony. Above all she felt good.

Back at Stewart's Grove, Hannah looked at herself critically in the mirror. The blue sweat suit no longer hung loosely on a skeletal frame. The humidity on the island was making her hair curl. She washed her hair and combed it out, then brushed it close to her head. Awful, she decided, fluffing it up. Even then it looked forlorn, but it was an improvement. She surveyed her face critically. She had to admit Arielle was beautiful; she, herself, would be lucky to make cute. So what? She had Greg. True, she wasn't a genius, and the boys hadn't flocked around her. But all she wanted was to be liked and to have a reasonably good time.

After breakfast she returned to her room to write to Melanie, just as the first warning drops began to patter on her window.

Stewart's Grove
July 10

Dear Melanie,

Greg is the most gorgeous, exciting guy in the world. He had a clambake on Mrs. Chase's beach. He picked me up in a Jeep with two of his friends, Keri and Steve. She's real cute and Steve looks a bit like Grumps (the doll, I mean, not Mrs. Pascoe).

Greg's old girlfriend showed up, and made all these catty remarks. He just ignored them, but if looks could kill, I wouldn't be writing this. She kept glaring at me, BUT I DIDN'T CARE. Aren't you proud of your weepy little friend?

To cut a long story short—HE KISSED ME!!!! I half expected it but didn't know what to do. I think I did it right.

Saturday we go to the fireworks display. It used to be on July 4, but this way, so Steve says, they can get two crowds of tourists. He has a boat, so we get to see the fireworks from the ocean.

But that isn't all. Weird things are happening at Stewart's Grove. I still have my dreams, though not so often.

Anyway when I went to bed after the clambake I couldn't sleep. Then I saw a light in Long Walk. SO I FOLLOWED IT. It was pitch black, and I had to edge my way along feeling for the statues.

The light disappeared into the oldest part of the house and guess what? After I nearly had a heart attack, it was GREG! He'd come to investigate my story of following a ghost down Long Walk.

It's raining again. Can you believe it? I thought the island was famous for good weather, but there's something called the temperature humidity index. It can get real sticky here, and then we get thunder and lightning.

Love ya always,
Hannah

P.S. I don't have a picture of Greg yet, but when I do *you will be the second to see it.*

Hannah left the letter by the hall stand. She had expected the rain to stop, but a constant drizzle set in; at last she realized there was no possibility of taking a walk that day and stayed in her room, out of Mrs. Donohue's way. Time passed quickly when she took up *Wuthering Heights*.

The following day it rained solidly. Hannah finished *Wuthering Heights* and began *Jane Eyre*. Saturday looked equally unpromising. "More rain," sniffed Mrs. Donohue at breakfast. "Weather's never been the same since they dropped those atomic bombs. Rain will ruin the fireworks."

Yet, just as Hannah was ready to accept this gloomy forecast, the sun began to banish the clouds. By ten, clear patches of sky had been stitched together to form one uninterrupted blue. Hannah decided to walk down to the beach.

When she left by the luggage door and stepped out from the shadow of Stewart's Grove, Hannah knew she had selected the right clothes for once. The sun's heat was almost palpable, and she was thankful she had on her yellow knit tank top and a pair of white shorts. On her feet were a pair of white leather Reeboks.

The cliff path was steep and narrow, not like the road, which took its time with a wide curve and slow descent. Cord grass scratched her legs; her feet pressed hard into the toes of her sneakers. From the top of the cliff, Vineyard Sound had looked unmoving and one blue-green color; but as she descended the noise of the waves and the cries of the gulls became louder, and the ocean broke up into white foam as it ran up the beach.

She almost ended at a run because the grade had become so steep; behind her pebbles showered down. Jumping the last three feet, she landed ankle deep in soft white sand. Hannah took off her Reeboks, stuffed her socks into them, knotted the laces together, and hung them around her neck. Walking along the edge of the ocean, she let the incoming tide lap over her feet.

Perhaps because she was concentrating on this amusement, it was some time before Hannah noticed a small catboat coming around the rocks at the south end of the beach. Keri was waving and shouting to attract her attention. Hannah waved back; the boat came closer inshore.

"Can you get to The Klothes Horse in Edgartown at two o'clock?" shouted Keri.

"Two o'clock," Hannah replied. "Sure!"

"Can't stop. We're racing to Gay Head," Keri yelled. "Don't forget the fireworks. Bring a swimsuit."

Steve was steering the boat. He and Keri waved and were soon gone. Behind them a dozen sailboats of various sizes and shapes were in hot pursuit.

Glancing at her watch, Hannah saw it was eleven-thirty. Turning, she walked back toward Stewart's Grove, choosing the longer route by the road rather than the cliff path.

Her journey took her past the walled herb garden. Through the gate she saw her aunt busily weeding. On seeing Hannah, Mrs. Chase straightened her back and sighed. "I'm not so young as I was, and there never was much joy in pulling weeds." Looking at her watch, she continued. "It will soon be time for lunch, I see. Let's rest a minute before we go in, shall we?"

There was a wrought-iron bench by the side of the path, and they sat together. The garden was set out like a giant spoked wheel, but octagonal rather than round. The spokes divided different beds of herbs from one another. Around the rim of the garden were flowers; Hannah recognized delphiniums, lupines, and marigolds. There were also a dozen smaller areas devoted to roses.

"Do you know anything about flowers?" asked Mrs. Chase.

"Not much," admitted Hannah.

"It's one of the great ironies of life," said her great-aunt. "When you have the energy to look after plants, you don't have much interest in them." Standing and pointing to a spindly green bush, she added, "That's basil. Keeps pests off tomatoes. In France they call it the royal herb."

Leading the way slowly along the path, she continued, "Everything here was used by the early settlers. Over

110

there"—she pointed with her trowel—"is lavender; that orange-yellow flower is calendula. The white one is caraway; its licorice taste made it useful for flavoring. And that's skunk cabbage, supposed to cure asthma, and next to it, the bright orange plant was called pleurisy root by the Indians. And that's santonica; its dried leaves were used for repelling moths and insects. Now smell these."

Eager to please her aunt, Hannah bent over a plant with clusters of buttonlike yellow flowers. Mrs. Chase broke off a stem. Hannah was instantly aware of a pungent aromatic smell. "They used it as a flavoring and for embalming; a peculiar mix, isn't it. Still, I'd rather be cured by herbs than some witch's brew of roasted toad powder."

Walking happily by her aunt's side, Hannah realized that it was possible for an adult to be shy. Mrs. Chase had lived alone for so long she probably was as nervous as Hannah when they met. That was something. Her aunt seemed so in control. Keri was right; you had to believe in yourself. And because Greg liked Hannah, she felt good about herself, and maybe others sensed it and were drawn more to her and confided more in her. Everything and everyone seemed tied together in some mysterious way. The answer was belief in herself, she decided. Together Hannah and Mrs. Chase left the herb garden through the gate and walked toward the front of Stewart's Grove.

"It's a pity the fountain isn't on," said Hannah. "It would be so pretty on a day like this."

"I ordered it turned off the day my husband died," said Mrs. Chase shortly. "It is a memory of a happy time. Perhaps one day I'll have it turned back on."

There was an embarrassed silence. Finally with an effort Mrs. Chase said, "I knew nothing about herbs or gardening when I started. Neither did Mr. Donohue. You can learn anything if you set your mind to it."

Luncheon was less strained than usual, though Mrs. Chase said little. Their conversation in the herb garden was the only time they had exchanged more than a few words. Hannah did learn that Mrs. Donohue was going to Edgartown that afternoon and asked for a ride.

Her request was grudgingly granted, and it meant listening to a monologue on the problems off-islanders brought to the Vineyard. Finally they passed the blinking light by the airport. "I'll let you off at the school parking lot," Mrs. Donohue said as they wove in and out of State Road traffic. "There's some silly nonsense going on there now, and I'm not going to take you downtown."

"The parking lot will be fine," Hannah assured her.

She was rewarded with a loud sniff.

The sky above the school football field was jammed with man-eating sharks, dragons, and brilliantly colored centipedes. Above them all was a string of box kites, some five or six in number, all attached to one thick rope. Dozens of kites rose briefly, twisted furiously a few feet from the grass, and fell; most never got airborne. Hannah had plenty of time to watch; three trolleys left before she could find a seat on one. It was jam-packed with people, many carrying the crushed remnants of paper and plastic kites. A young man next to her said proudly, "I won a prize last year for 'First Kite to Become Tangled Inextricably with Another.' This year I may win for 'First in a Tree.' I'm going to the kite shop to buy another—just in case."

Hannah realized that every time she came to Edgartown the streets were more crowded than ever. The summer people came in endless numbers. Ferries delivered them hour after hour, and those who didn't go to the beach wandered aimlessly about looking for something to do or somewhere to go.

The shopping and dining center of Edgartown was clustered around the waterfront because no food was permitted on the beach, just where the crowds were thickest. The shops were an interesting mix, a store selling live sand eels was next to a fashion boutique. Beside the boutique was a takeout place for fried clams.

Since she was a little early, Hannah had time on her hands. Looking into the stores, she worked her way slowly down Main Street.

There was a gift shop selling nothing but scrimshaw. A meticulously executed scene of early whaling ships at sea carved on a whale's tooth caught her eye—until she saw the price.

When she arrived at The Klothes Horse, Hannah looked through the beach wear. Nothing appealed to her.

Keri arrived fifteen minutes late, out of breath, and making excuses for her tardiness. "Off-islanders, everywhere. It's like a swarm of locusts. The kite-flying competition brings them out. Steve went up there." She paused to catch her breath, then continued. "He thinks he's going to win first prize for 'Most Island-Oriented Kite.' Oh boy!" She looked around, poked at a bikini, and held the top in front of her. "This would drive Steve wild." Throwing it carelessly to one side, she took Hannah's arm. "Come on. This is all junk."

They left; the sales assistant, who was painting her toenails purple, didn't even look up.

"How did you do in the sailboat race?" Hannah asked now she could get a word in.

"Third prize in our class. Another tin cup for Steve's collection; he's already filled one display cabinet. Boy, talk about competitive."

"What's his kite like?"

"Like?"

"You said it was island oriented."

"Oh, sure. It's shaped like a big wine bottle and is three feet long exactly. Get it? Wine equals vine and three feet equals a—"

"Yard," Hannah finished.

"Exactly. Too subtle for the judges, probably. Anyway, it flew about two feet, then buried itself in the sand. Let's get a Coke; he'll be busy for a while."

Keri steered Hannah down a narrow alley and they were soon inside the narrowest building Hannah had ever seen. "Behold, 'The Thin Malt Shoppe,' " Keri announced.

"You don't think Steve will win, then," said Hannah when they were seated at a tiny round table.

Keri sucked on her straw, gazing thoughtfully at the ceiling. "Well, there is a prize for 'Most Up and Down Kite'; one thing's for sure, he'll win something. But he'll have a harder time getting by these tables."

They both erupted into laughter, then got the giggles and were still acting silly when Steve squeezed into the store. His T-shirt, stretched to its limits, proudly proclaimed "Runner Up: Kite That Never Left the Ground." Again the girls dissolved into hysterical laughter. Steve looked at them and shook his head. "Women," he muttered, "all crazy. Come on, Greg will be waiting."

Hannah suddenly felt very nervous about meeting Greg. She was afraid he might find her shallow. Keri assumed that she was now his girlfriend, but was she? They had never really been on a date together, and he was two years older than she. Probably he thought of her as a dumb off-islander who needed guidance at every turn. But there was the kiss; that surely meant something. A boy like Greg probably kissed lots of girls; he'd certainly kissed Arielle. But it was not Arielle who was going out with him now. Hannah had to remember Melanie's advice: "Forget that little voice of doubt. Self-confidence is the key."

When they reached *The Siren* Greg waved to them. He was wearing blue shorts, a T-shirt, and deck shoes. As he was helping Hannah aboard, their eyes met, and he grinned. His hair was held in place by a peaked cap. The boat was rocked by a sudden swell, and Greg had to steady her in his arms. She felt suddenly very shy and self-conscious and muttered, "Sorry." When she looked around Keri and Steve were both grinning. This time she knew she blushed.

The boat was a streamlined craft, white with blue trim, and over them was a canopy. There were two seats in the pilot-house and two small louvered doors leading down to a cabin. From it came frenzied barking mixed with piteous whining. In the stern, there was a bench seat. Steve took the driver's seat. "Quiet down, Wipeout," he shouted, "or it's the pound for you."

Keri helped Hannah fasten her life jacket. "Greg likes you," she whispered. "Me too. Thank the Lord we're free of Arielle B-W. She hated the ocean. Can you imagine it? Dating a marine biologist when you hate the sea?" They struggled briefly with the straps. "Arielle got seasick every time we left the dock. She came anyway. You don't get sick, do you?" Reaching into a side pocket of the boat, she took out a cap. "Put this on, it keeps the sun off. Loop the strap under your hair, or it will blow away at the first gust of wind."

Greg had stepped ashore and was untying the short ropes

holding *The Siren* to the dock. He tossed them aboard, and Keri tied them off.

From the driver's seat, Steve asked over his shoulder, "Everyone okay?" Then he turned the key in the ignition, and the engine roared into life. "Are we clear bow and stern?"

"All clear," said Greg, taking his place next to Hannah.

Steve moved the selector into drive; the engine revolutions increased. He turned the wheel gently as they moved out from the dock. Then, with a roar, the boat was surging across the bay toward the line of buoys marking the harbor limits.

The ocean was as busy as Main Street; Steve skillfully maneuvered them through traffic until they were safe beyond the buoys.

"Let him out," said Steve, in a resigned tone.

Greg opened the little door that led to the cabin and galley; there was a loud bark of joy, and Wipeout shot up the little companionway, gave a quick yelp of recognition at seeing them, and dived over the side.

"Crazy dog," Steve said, shaking his head. "Absolutely crazy," he added, swinging the boat to starboard.

"That's the same thing as chasing cars on land," Keri told Hannah, "except he's not as likely to get run over. We can go on now; he's got it out of his system."

It was Greg who leaned over the stern of the boat and hauled Wipeout aboard. To show his gratitude, the dog shook himself dry, covering the four of them with cold drops of water.

A line of buoys and a police cutter, its blue light circling, marked the fireworks viewing anchorage. Steve effortlessly brought the boat into position. "There's the launching platform," he said, pointing. "And now we wait," he added, throwing the anchor overboard. "Last year there were a thousand boats here by sunset. One thing all fireworks shows have in common is they last a few minutes, but you wait forever. But the early bird gets the best view." He looked around and seemed satisfied. "We don't want to be next to any gaff-rigged catboats even in this light chop. I want to watch the fireworks, not some wild swinging boom."

He had his fishing rod and seemed content to sit with a chicken sandwich while waiting for a fish to take the bait. The others swam near the boat. Keri found an opportunity to whisper to Hannah: "Greg likes the way you look in that swimsuit." She might have said more, but at that moment Wipeout jumped into the water near her, and she gulped a mouthful of salt water. She was still spluttering when Steve called them in to fix dinner. He'd caught nothing. "All that swimming scared the fish. I caught a thirty-pound striped bass here last year," he commented morosely. Keri indicated a length of three inches with her hands, but fortunately Steve was too disconsolate to notice.

Their meal consisted of hot dogs cooked in a skillet and they ate it with all four of them, along with the restless Wipeout, squashed into the tiny cabin.

At last, to the west, thin bands of clouds extending across the path of the setting sun became gradually invisible as the sky darkened from blue to purple. The water was smoothed by a light northerly wind.

"Look at that," said Steve in awe. From one boat a kite had been launched with a string of light sticks. "And I couldn't get mine off the ground," he added ruefully.

Keri kissed him on the cheek. "It flew once; don't forget that."

"Six feet two inches, that's all. Still," he added, brightening, "I have another T-shirt."

All the boats had turned their running lights on: red for port, green for starboard. A few added white taillights. The only sound was that of water lapping against hulls and masts creaking in the wind. Excitement gripped the spectators.

"Won't be long now," said Keri.

"I'll believe that when—"

Just as Steve spoke, the first rocket whooshed upward, splitting into a thousand colored lights above the water and the floating town. The sound of music blasted across the harbor from the launching platform. There was more blaring of ship horns when the music to *Jaws* was played. After that came the music to *Les Miserables*. A hundred rockets soared into the blackness, only to lose their momentum and fall back in great exploding bouquets of red, green, and blue. As one fell, another rose to take its place, perfectly choreographed, and the sky was never without a riot of ever-changing color. Greg had his arm around Hannah. *I wish this night could go on forever,* she thought.

But finally Neil Diamond was singing *America*, and for the whole three minutes the sky became a glittering gold Milky Way. Then there was silence.

The moment passed; with a frenzy of starters, engines sprang into life. Horns blasted the air as the boats edged clear of one another. The police cutters began shepherding their flock toward the harbor. "You can let that mutt out now," said Steve. "Just tell him to behave himself."

Wipeout had been locked in the cabin for most of the show, not because he was frightened by the fireworks, but because he barked back at them.

"Are you going to see *A Midsummer Night's Dream*?" asked Keri as Steve, with Greg's help, worked *The Siren* in and out of the armada.

"Aunt Caroline said something about going," Hannah replied. "I really like Shakespeare. Are you?"

"Am I? My dear child, I'm in it. You're looking at Helena. I haven't learned all those lines for nothing."

"Boooring," Steve said, avoiding a catboat that seemed determined to ram them.

"Are you going, Greg?" Hannah asked, tentatively.

"I'd like to," he said, using the boat hook to fend off the catboat. "But I've got to go to Amherst to fix up my fall classes."

"Likely story," said Steve. "I suppose I'll have to put in an appearance."

"The boy has no culture," Keri added in a loud stage whisper to Hannah. " 'But God made him, let him pass for a man.' "

For Hannah, when she heard Greg say he was leaving, all the pleasure went out of the evening. She sat in the stern of the boat not noticing anything around her.

Hannah heard a wave slap against the boat and felt a sudden tightness in her stomach. The knot grew tighter. Her heart pounded, something filled her throat, she gasped for air, falling forward onto the wooden deck of *The Siren*. Someone was screaming a long, long way off. Suddenly she doubled over, arms crossed, as if to ward off a terrible blow. Then pain erupted from inside her body, as if a red-hot wire were being drawn through the marrow of her bones. The scream came closer; pain seized her, shook her like a rag doll, and threw her to the deck.

119

She was the one screaming, and her back was on fire. With a wrenching effort, Hannah opened her eyes.

Greg was holding her; the other two were staring at her with frightened eyes.

"What happened?" she asked in panic. "My back, it's on fire."

Keri pulled the top of Hannah's shirt down. There was a livid red mark.

Hannah closed her eyes and then reopened them. The pain was localized in her left shoulder.

"My shoulder."

Greg's voice was tense. "It looks like a branding iron touched it. There's a bright red burn mark here."

The pain lessened. Drained of strength, Hannah sat on the deck, supported by Greg. She couldn't see anything clearly; there wasn't a sound. She tried moving her arms and legs; they responded. She became aware of noises all around her; at first they were indistinct, then she picked up on the tone of anxiety in the words. Then three faces came into focus, anxious, concerned.

Managing a weak smile, she said, "I'm fine. Just help me to my seat."

"It might have been a jellyfish," Greg said doubtfully. "The red part has almost disappeared. There's a sort of bruise with yellow around the edges. Some jellyfish can cause a delayed reaction."

"A Portuguese man-of-war," suggested Steve.

"I don't think so. The sting doesn't go away that quickly." He stopped, then added in amazement, "It's vanished; there's no mark now."

Steve had stopped the boat; a police cutter was heading toward them. "Should she go to the hospital?" he asked.

"No! No! I'm fine. Just get me back to the house."

In the Jeep little was said. Steve and Keri sat in the back, but there wasn't any of the usual good humor. Hannah found the silence depressing, especially because she was the cause of it.

At the luggage door moths fluttered around the small outside light. Greg put his arms around her, and he whispered, "You really scared me. Don't do that again," as his hands gently brushed her hair.

This time their kiss was long. The pleasure spread from Hannah's lips through her whole body. "I'll miss you while I'm at Amherst," he said.

Her eyes searched his face, then she put her head on his shoulder. They stayed like that for a long time, each holding the other, thinking private thoughts and saying nothing.

Part 2
A Witch Across Time

10
Patience Cory

DR. MARSH, WEARING A CHECKED SHIRT AND KHAKI pants, was waiting for Hannah by the door. Her reading glasses hung from a black strap around her neck. In her hand was the inevitable pack of sugarless gum. They went down to the consulting room.

Hannah took the canvas chair; the doctor shut the drapes and sat in her chair and moved the little table to one side. The only illumination came from the lamp behind the doctor; the humming of the air conditioner was barely audible.

"Hannah," said Dr. Marsh, "I'm going to review briefly what hypnotism is, and then I shall put you into a trance and go backward into your childhood to see if I can uncover any deep emotional trauma. You won't feel any pain or discomfort."

"Fine," said Hannah, feeling rather nervous nevertheless.

"Are you comfortable?"

"Yes."

"No drafts? It's not too hot?"

"No."

The doctor reached into her purse and took out a slim silver tube. "This is a penlight, Hannah." There was a slight click, and the bulb at the end of the pen glowed. "In a minute, I shall ask you to look at it."

"I understand."

"The purpose of hypnotism is to bring out those fears everyone tries to hide from others and themselves. I shall take you back through the years to your childhood in an effort to discover what lies deep in your subconscious and to find some reason for the dreams you keep having."

She extinguished the desk lamp; the only illumination was the pinpoint in the air, some eighteen inches away from Hannah's face. "Please look at the penlight."

The doctor's voice, low and soothing, came out of the darkness. Hannah could see only a smudge of face behind the single eye of light.

"Soon you will be between sleep and wakefulness, but I do not want you to go to sleep. Later you may sleep, but not now. Soon you will be in a state where you dream and know you are dreaming. Nod if you understand."

Hannah nodded.

"Now I want you to focus on the tiny light and take five deep breaths. Let them come from the depths of your lungs and feel the air as it is drawn in through your body."

She did as asked. The light remained like a star in the blackness of space.

"Keep your eyes on the penlight. You will see that it is really two lights. The center is much brighter than the edge. It is a glowing heart. Focus on it."

Hannah stared at the light; it had a life of its own; the intensity varied; now it was more like a flame than a bulb.

"I am going to count. When I count 'one' you will close your eyes, but you will see the light in your imagination. You will still focus on the brightest part of the light. And while I talk you will become sleepier. And sleepier. The light means sleep. The light means sleep."

Hannah could hear nothing but Dr. Marsh's voice and see nothing but the pen shining in a void.

"The light means sleep. Sleep and light. Sleep, light. When I count 'two' you may open your eyes and look directly at the light. Just looking at the brightness makes you more sleepy than ever. The light is sleep. The flame is a signal for you to sleep. You will drift into a pleasant, relaxing sleep.

"And soon I will reach a count of three. You will close your eyes and pick up the image of the light in your mind again. Now you will be very, very sleepy. You will keep your eyes closed and drift into a deep, pleasant, relaxing sleep, and we will talk."

"One."

Hannah's eyes closed.

"Two."

Hannah's eyes opened.

"Three."

They closed.

Dr. Marsh counted slowly until she reached the number ten. Then she turned the penlight off and put it quietly on the table.

"Hannah. You can hear nothing but my voice. Your eyelids are very heavy. Even if you try to open them, you cannot. I will tell you when to open them. You cannot open them. The harder you try, the tighter they remain closed.

127

They are glued together. Try to open them, and you will see you cannot."

The eyes remained firmly shut.

"Now I'm going to lift your arm; you will not be able to hold your arm up because it is so heavy. It is heavy and you are too tired."

Gently Dr. Marsh reached for Hannah's arm and raised it. The arm slowly returned to Hannah's lap.

"Your name is Hannah?"

"Hannah Kincaid."

"You are living on the island now?"

"Yes."

"With your great-aunt, Caroline Chase?"

"Yes."

"Do you go to school?"

"Vacation."

"Before the vacation."

"Reach Out Academy."

"Hannah, I want to go back to the time before you went to Reach Out."

Hannah became uneasy; she shifted in the armchair and appeared to be on the brink of speaking. Dr. Marsh's voice was soothing. "Your mother was a lawyer, wasn't she?"

"Yes."

"And your father is an engineer?"

"Yes."

"And you lived in Ohio?"

"Yes."

Dr. Marsh paused, waiting a few moments until she was certain Hannah had settled into a deep trance.

"You did things with your mother?"

"We went shopping a lot. . . . Daddy said we would put him in the poorhouse."

"You enjoyed this time with your mother?"

"Dead now." Hannah stirred uneasily.

Dr. Marsh, realizing she had come too close to the accident, said softly, "I want to go back in time. Before the accident, before high school, before junior high."

"Yes."

"You went to grade school in Sylvania, Ohio?"

"Yes."

"Who sits in front of you?"

"Jacqueline McHugh."

"What is your best subject?"

"English."

"What are you reading?"

"Not reading."

"All right, all right. In English class, what is the teacher's name?"

"Mrs. Bouve."

"Is she old?"

"Yes. About forty."

"We are going even further back, Hannah. We're going back to the time when you were six. When I talk to you, you will be a first grader. Now you are six years old, but you can still answer my questions."

"Who sits in front of you in the first-grade room?"

"No one." Astonishingly, Hannah's voice had become that of a child, clear and small.

"No one? Why does no one sit in front of you?"

"Front row."

Dr. Marsh smiled in spite of the seriousness of the situation.

Hannah answered questions with the same childlike intensity. She was gently led to her kindergarten days. Asked who sat on each side of her she could still recall the names Paul and Janet. She did not know their last names. Her teacher was a Miss Norman.

"Who is your best friend?"

"Susie."

"Susie what?"

Hannah frowned, her face wrinkled in an exaggerated effort to remember.

"Ingersoll."

"Rest and relax. I will not ask you any more questions for a while. But I want you to think about what I am saying. You are going back . . . back . . . You are now four years old. Think about that. Think about some scene when you were four years old."

Hannah appeared to be struggling to say something.

"You don't have to tell me about it. Just think about it and see yourself at that age. Now go back a year. You are three years old. See yourself. See some scene when you were three years old. Think about a toy or dress you had when you were three years old.

"Bubbles," came the response. "Bubbles."

"Yes, Bubbles. Bubbles was your friend. You loved Bubbles."

"Yes. Bubbles my dolly. We got spanked."

"Why was that?"

"We scraped paint off the bed."

"Why?"

"Mad at Mama. She made me eat spinach."

"And Bubbles helped?"

"Yes."

130

The doctor smiled again. "Now I want you to go back another year. You are two. Two years old. Two years old. See a scene and imagine yourself in the scene."

"Cottage."

"You have a cottage?"

"By sea."

"What did you do?"

"Built castle in sand. But . . ." her voice trailed off.

"Yes?"

"Whiskers spoil it."

"You have a dog as a pet?"

"No. Cat." Her voice was lisping and uncertain.

Further and further Dr. Marsh went, in hope of finding some deeply rooted cause of Hannah's dreams.

"Hannah, you are one year old. You ask for a drink of water. What do you say?"

"Wa. Wa." It took a tremendous effort. There was a long pause. "Mama. Wa. Wa."

Dr. Marsh sat back in her chair. This was enough for one session. "Hannah," she said. "Rest and relax, and when I tell you to wake up you may do so. You will hear my voice, but you will do nothing until I tell you to wake up. I will snap my fingers and you will awaken. Not until then. Do you understand?"

Hannah said nothing; Dr. Marsh looked closely into her face. Hannah stirred uneasily; a moan escaped from her lips. She struggled in the chair, clenching and unclenching her fists.

"Patience Cory," Hannah said suddenly, and in a slightly different accent. "Patience Cory."

The doctor drew back, astonished and alarmed. She made the instant decision not to risk bringing Hannah out of her trance. The only safe procedure was to allow Hannah to continue. "Who is Patience Cory, Hannah?"

"Me."

"You are Patience?"

"Patience Cory."

"All right, all right. Where do you live?"

"On the island. Cory's Creek, near Tisbury."

"And where do you go to school?"

"No school. Fifteen. I can read, though. I read my Bible all the time. I have my own Bible, read it always while baking."

"What do you bake?"

"Bread. Corn cake, plump, golden, crisp around edges. Apple pie."

"What is the kitchen like?"

"'Tis a lot of work. The floor must be sanded, hearthstone polished, and pewter pots scoured with sand. Why do you ask questions? Who are you?"

"Patience, I am Lucetta Marsh, a friend."

Dr. Marsh's face was close to Hannah's, betraying none of the anxiety she was feeling. Something was terribly wrong, and she dared not force the issue by trying to bring Hannah out of her trance. The only solution was to follow where Hannah led. "What day is it?"

"Sabbath."

"Where are you going today?"

"Service."

"What is the minister's name?"

"Minister Slaughter."

"Did you attend service last Sunday?"

"Yes."

"With your family?"

"Not Pa. Minister Slaughter doesn't like him. Pa never goes to the service. Some say he be a Quaker."

"Is that bad?"

"Yes, Ma feared for his soul."

"What is your mother's name?"

"Prudence. She died of the plague five years ago."

"What year is it?"

"1692 in the Year of Our Lord."

"Patience, are you telling me the truth?"

"I'm a good girl." The tone was shocked.

"All right. All right. You always tell the truth or God would punish you."

"I tell the truth because it is God's commandment."

"Do you have brothers and sisters?"

"Sister."

"Do you have uncles and aunts?"

"Think so."

"You are not sure?"

Silence. Hannah sat completely relaxed, hands lightly clasped in her lap.

"All right. All right. Do you have any relatives besides your sister?"

"No. Sister married. She lives on mainland. It's two days' ride after ferry."

"Does she dress like you?"

"Yes."

"I want you—"

Suddenly, with a fearful, low intensity, the voice said, "There be witches. Witches!"

11

Matthew Beverley

"WITCHES?"

"Aye, witches! . . ."

The widow Proctor's cow, Marigold, died. Men tried to get her to her feet, but she could not move. They dug a hole and buried her where she'd dropped. Goody Proctor said there had been blood in the beast's milk for two days.

A day later the Reverend Slaughter's sow farrowed six piglets, one of them with two heads. And everyone knew it was a sign.

Within a week, the village was wracked by torments. Men and women suffered hideous convulsive fits brought on by witches and demons. Several hayricks were scattered, and the children who were present saw a tall man in a black cloak laughing at the sight.

Goodwife Martin was walking through the woods when a

large striped cat stopped in her path, its glass-green eyes fixed unblinkingly upon her. When she moved to go around it, the creature arched its back, its fur sticking up like porcupine quills. She closed her eyes and prayed; when she opened them again, the beast had vanished into the air.

Soon after, Goodwife Martin lost her power of speech; her throat contracted rapidly and continually, a sure sign that demons were attempting to make her swallow devilish poisons. Samuel Cleary was the first in the village of Tisbury to die. Soon after, the newborn child of the constable died.

The minister did what he could. Over a period of two weeks, he preached ten sermons in Chilmark and six in Tisbury on the evils of witches.

Most piteous of all were the afflicted children. James Seaton and his cousin Deliverance fell in fits. Deliverance was thought to be with child by Satan. Both claimed they saw a great black wart upon the thigh of Agnes Preston, and it was discovered when she was searched, though it disappeared immediately after. When Minister Slaughter attempted to bless Deliverance, she tossed in agony. Her legs flailed madly, and her back bent so far that only her heels and the back of her head touched the bed. Minister Slaughter reckoned her spine to be two feet above the bed. This position she held for fully ten minutes before collapsing. Then she gave a long, pitiful groan and was still.

Thomas Avery, a servant to William Stewart, most prosperous of the villagers, claimed that the night before, when the moon was full, Mary Leacock had appeared to him and made a lewd suggestion that he indignantly refused. Mary was taken up and lodged in the jail.

Jennet Law, an old, ugly woman living on the outskirts of

the village, was accused of giving the evil eye to several village elders and the minister himself. Jennet was arrested, to the relief of many. But she did not go willingly.

"Damn you all," she screamed. "You'll all burn in hell for this."

"Not before you do," Josiah Bailey, the jailer, told her grimly. "'Tis you and your Satan's spawn brought about the death of my poor child."

Witch marks were found upon Jennet's body and a secret teat with which she suckled Satan and his imps. She had a familiar spirit in the shape of a large tabby cat called Felix. Priscilla East claimed the creature could turn into an owl at night. She had seen the cat in the forest one night; then it was gone, and she heard the hooting of an owl.

Samuel Callcott, returning one evening from drinking with four companions, was greeted by Susannah Swinton, with whom he had kept company until she could stand his carousing no longer. She came in ghostly form and gloated over him. That night he was so sick his life was despaired of. Susannah Swinton was taken up.

Minister Slaughter was called to the house of Judith McKay. She had lain on her bed without food for seven days.

"Why Judith, what ails you?" asked the minister, not approaching too closely, for witches could jump great distances.

"I cannot swallow," the girl replied weakly.

"'Tis true," her mother agreed. "She has scarce swallowed one morsel of food, and though she took some hard cider it rather increased her hunger than broke her fast."

The minister nodded wisely. "Sometimes a chestnut or a little cold water will go down. Perhaps a little gruel or porridge."

136

While the minister waited, Judith's mother prepared a bowl of porridge, but when she attempted to spoon it into her daughter's mouth, the girl set her teeth on edge and was thrown into such hideous torments she threatened to fly from the bed. Witch wounds in the form of bloody hand prints appeared on her arms.

When Judith lay calm again, the minister, with the help of her father, managed with the greatest difficulty to remove four pins and a nail from Judith's mouth. The marks on her arms vanished as quickly as they had appeared.

Minister Slaughter spoke with Judith's father as they went for the preacher's horse. "She's bewitched, no question. The witch wounds and the pins prove that. When did the torments commence?"

Joshua McKay passed a hand wearily over his face; the gesture showed the exhaustion of seven nights without sleep. "It began soon after she and Jared Cheever stopped walking out. We all thought they were to be wed. She's a fine strong girl—or she was. She could have given him many children. But no tokens were exchanged, and young people are fickle."

The horse was drinking quietly from a wooden trough near the small barn. Joshua patted its neck, speaking softly as he walked it back to its master. "Jared walks out with Patience Cory now, I hear," he added, handing the horse's bridle to the minister.

"I hear he does." There was an awkward silence. The minister cleared his throat, then returned to Judith's torment. "It began with visions, no doubt."

"Aye. She saw specters. We were told to make as if to strike her eyes, and when we did, it would not make her blink. She hears nothing most of the time because her ears are wholly taken up by invisible assailants. I have sometimes hallooed loudly in her ears, but the poor child hears naught of it."

While Joshua steadied the horse, Reverend Slaughter placed a foot in the stirrup and swung himself into the saddle. "These are testing times, brother, and we must not cease vigilance. I've taken a step not yet ready to be revealed which, with God's grace, will help rid us of witches." Taking the bridle, he turned his horse's head and added, "Keep watch. The demons come when we sleep. And let no woman save your wife near Judith as you prize her immortal soul."

Kicking his heels, the minister urged his horse in the direction of the village.

A week passed; there were no new cases. Judith McKay regained her wits and was able to take a little broth. James Seaton and Deliverance were no longer afflicted; the swelling disappeared from Deliverance's belly.

There was a gathering at the church to discuss releasing the witches. At least twenty women and two men were now lodged in the tiny jail, and Mary Leacock had a fever that was likely to spread to the others. The men and a dozen of the women were released; the remainder were not so fortunate.

The Reverend Slaughter was opposed to giving them their freedom; he had much support. Others were not so sure. Jared Cheever, a youth of eighteen with a strong jaw and sea-green eyes, showed little fear of Minister Slaughter or his friends. Many a maiden present knew there was no one more handsome in doublet and breeches.

Facing the crowded benches, Jared spoke. "What first roused this talk of witches?" He looked around. No one answered. "I'll tell ye, neighbors. It was envy, backbiting, and gossip." There was a buzz of agreement which was quickly drowned by protests. "Let me be heard," Jared continued, raising his hand for silence. "I ask only that courtesy."

The congregation became quiet.

"Someone complains his bread will not rise or his cream become butter. Witchcraft, they claim. Is it likely the Devil, or any of his minions, would stoop to concern themselves with the fate of a New England loaf or cow?"

Several voices cried "Sit down," and one or two "Blasphemy." Others, however, voiced their support.

"It is not blasphemy to question the credulous. Perhaps we are too ready to cast stones. What are these charges against witches? Some hysterical children topple a rick and in fear say Satan was the cause. Some disappointed wooer sees his mistress in a drunken vision . . ."

There was an uproar at this. To his credit, Samuel Callcott did not join in but hung his head. "And," continued Jared, his voice raised above the hubbub, "when a free person can go to jail because a child sees a cat go into the forest and hears an owl hoot, things have come to a pretty pass indeed." He sat down. A few of those who had urged him to hold his peace looked less certain.

The minister held both hands up for silence. "We thank Jared Cheever for his opinions. We are a free people within the sight of God." There was a murmur of agreement. One or two smiled at Jared as if relieved that he had had his say and the real business of the meeting could continue. "There are some who feel, like Jared, the witches should be released," he continued. There was a loud hissing and two or three of the congregation shook their fists angrily.

Patience looked at Jared's face. There was determination there and honesty and decency. No one had been more surprised than she when he had visited her house some three weeks ago and asked to see her father.

All day she had been making candles. It was messy work and trying too, for the fire had to be kept going and the candle rods constantly dipped, allowed to cool, then brought back until the wax fattened slowly into hard slow-burning candles.

At last the first batch was ready. Patience had washed her hands clean and, while supper was cooking, had taken up her Bible when she heard the knock. Setting the book on the edge of the great stone hearth, she opened the door. Her confusion at seeing Jared was acute, and she was painfully aware of blushing crimson as he entered. They stood in the center of the room, awkwardly trying to make conversation. Mercifully, her father came in from the barn, and she retired to the bedroom and left them alone.

Patience was astonished when her father told her the reason for Jared's visit.

"He asked to be allowed to walk out with you."

"Walk out with me?" asked Patience, faintly.

"It's up to you," replied her father. "Jared has my approval, but I'll not force any daughter of mine to keep company with anyone she dislikes. And then there's the family's reputation to think of."

Patience blushed again and looked quickly away; only at the last did she realize her father had been jesting. What better prospect was there for a son-in-law than Jared Cheever?

Now, as Patience looked at Jared across the room, she prayed he was thinking of her in a special way. Then, guiltily, she turned her attention back to Minister Slaughter.

He was pounding on his lecture stand; Patience heard his

final words: ". . . signs. These are the signs of witches, and I ask any man here to deny them."

There were muttered ayes and much pious nodding. "Satan has sent his agents to destroy our crops, cause famine and disease. But we shall weed them out like tares and torment them as they torment us!"

Though they sat in God's house, the villagers were so taken with the Reverend Slaughter's words that they rose and applauded vigorously. None of the elders tried to stop them.

Jared bided his time. When order was restored, he stood up slowly. "I do not take up for witches," he began. Several members of the congregation scoffed at this. "I grant things happen which God would not normally permit."

"Aye! Aye!" responded his opponents.

"He destroys his own argument," shouted William Dudley from the rear of the meetinghouse.

"But," continued Jared, "I question the evidence of children and those who love the pot with the long neck almost as much as their prayers."

There was a great deal of laughter at this. Samuel Callcott rose in confusion, thrusting his way from the church.

"Why do these children act as they do?" demanded Minister Slaughter.

"You must ask them," Jared replied. "Perhaps they like to be the center of attention. Perhaps the very fear of witchcraft itself is sufficient. . . ."

"What about the pins and nails my child vomited up?" demanded Joshua McKay. "What of them?"

It was some time before calm could be restored. Even then there was a restless uneasiness that would not be stilled.

"I say this," Jared told him. "If the minister, on his honor, will tell us of any case where a nail or pin was taken from an afflicted person's mouth in court with witnesses present, I will sit down and speak no more of this."

"Tell him, Reverend Slaughter," demanded a score of confident voices. "Aye, tell him."

All eyes now turned to the minister. His hands nervously clenched the edge of the lectern. An agonizing silence followed. Finally he admitted, "I cannot, on my honor."

Cries of dismay greeted his words. Jared sat down.

The door at the rear of the church was flung open. There in the entrance stood a tall man, a broad-brimmed beaver hat in hand. He wore leather boots, a doublet of dark blue with a falling band-linen ruffle, and cuffs of purest white. Without waiting to be introduced, he strode to the front. The Reverend Slaughter hastened to greet him.

"Brother Beverley," he said. "You've come at last to deliver us."

The name "Beverley" ran through the assembly. The man who stood before them stroking his jet black beard and fixing them with cold ice-blue eyes was none other than Matthew Beverley himself. The very name of the witch hunter sent a chill through men's hearts.

Even Jared felt the man's awesome presence, his magnetic appeal. Any thought of releasing the witches, had it been realistic, was banished forever. Minister Slaughter had intended to introduce his guest, but no such courtesy was required. Who had not heard of the works of Matthew Beverley? Five witches found in Nantucket Island and hanged, four in Boston. And in England he and the earl of Warwick had hanged a hundred or more. Was not Matthew Beverley the man who devised the famous system of watching witches for days and nights until finally their familiar spirits appeared?

Not a few in that church trembled for their souls. They were not witches, but they knew their unworthiness. A person could sin and sometimes not be aware of it. This was the man to ferret it out.

"There are witches in this very place of God," Beverley said, without preamble. "I sense their devilish presence. And also I sense many who are tormented by them." He approached Jared and fixed his eye upon him. "And do not doubt the existence of witches, for the Bible enjoins us not to suffer them to live. Any man who does not believe in witches is an heretic." Jared stood his ground, looking the man in the eye, and in the end it was Matthew Beverley who looked away.

Every one present felt the witch finder was talking to him personally. "They are as wicked as a witch and as guilty. Any means are permitted to make a witch confess, for witches cannot be sentenced unless they first confess."

A collective shudder ran around the room. So he had brought the instruments of torture with him. Not a few felt the urge to cross themselves in the old way, but to do so would open them to charges of being of the Popish heresy.

Matthew Beverley walked slowly to the front of the church, to stand beside Minister Slaughter.

"We are living in what were once the Devil's territories. The savages who live nearby are demons personified," Beverley informed them in harsh tones. "They paint their faces like devils and worship spirits and demons."

Jared rose slowly; Beverley's gaze fell upon him. "Yes, brother."

"But cannot the Devil come in any person's form, without his consent, and afflict someone?"

Beverley did not answer at first; he was removing his great gloves in a slow, almost hypnotic fashion. Only when he had placed them on the end of a bench did he speak. "Not without their consent. If a person be afflicted and can name the specter that torments him, it must reveal its guilt."

A murmur of assent arose. If the more thoughtful members of the congregation were alarmed, they kept their thoughts to themselves.

"Then, by your words," argued Jared, "any person could claim to be bewitched by someone and that would be taken as evidence."

"It would. And of guilt. For no one would accuse another falsely, since God would know of it and punish him in ways we cannot imagine."

"But," Jared replied, "I see little evidence of witchcraft."

"Evidence!" roared Beverley. "Evidence, young man? You have much to learn; the evidence is all around thee. Have there not been crop failures, storms, plagues of locusts and tent caterpillars? Has not one in this village died? Have not others suffered disease and wasting sicknesses? Did such things come from God?" Sensing he had the support of almost everyone present, he added triumphantly, "When you have lived as long as I have, you will know more of the wiles of the Devil and his harlots, those we call witches."

"Aye," said Simon Gleason. "Did not Susannah Swinton own a great cat? When she served as midwife to my Agnes did we not lose that child? Sickly he was and died because she inflicted it with a fit."

"Answer that," demanded several voices at the same time.

There was a disturbance at the back of the hall. Joshua

144

McKay came forward, thrusting his daughter before him. Judith's face was white as a sheet.

"My daughter is bewitched," said Joshua. "Many a morning she can scarce get out of bed. She vomits up pins. Today she started again." Reaching into a bag he had with him, he produced several tenpenny nails, handing them to the witch finder.

Beverley held them at a distance as if they were poisonous reptiles. "Ah. Now we have them." His stare fell upon Judith; she fell to her knees. "You wish to confess. Are you afflicted?" His eyes measured the weeping girl from head to toe. Narrowing his gaze, he growled. "Well?"

"I saw witchcraft," she muttered.

"Speak up, child." He put his hand under her chin, raising her up. "Tell everyone."

"I . . . I saw witchcraft," Judith said nervously.

"Yes. Do not be afraid, for none here can hurt thee."

"I rode upon a horse," she said, going grotesquely through the motions of riding a horse. "To a dark place. There were twelve witches present and the Devil."

From the congregation there arose several shrieks; many had fallen to their knees. Loud sobs could be heard.

"Aye," said Beverley, "for thirteen makes a fine coven."

"He had great horns," continued Judith, her matter-of-fact tone contrasting strangely with the horror of her tale. "And a great book. He said he would show me a way to fly."

Patience felt the oppressiveness of the heat in the church. The windows were firmly shut. She could barely concentrate as Judith's story continued.

"He took the fat of a dead child—" She was interrupted by cries of horror and more weeping from the congregation. "—which was seethed in a brass vessel, to this was added herbs and soot, and last the blood of bats. This the witches did anoint themselves with until they were red as savages. By this means, said the Devil, they could fly through the air and gain the heart of those they love."

"And what did the Devil ask of you?"

"To deny God." There were groans from the congregation. Her father fell to his knees, his hands raised before him in prayer. Others followed suit.

"To blaspheme. To murder children." Judith was forced to raise her voice above the uproar. "To promise my children to him. To worship him."

"And what did the Prince of Darkness promise you?" demanded Beverley.

"If I would sign his book in blood, I should have the heart of the one I love." Here she stole a glance in Jared's direction, but he was on his knees, deep in prayer. "And I should have anything my heart desired, and my soul would be his at my death. He held out a pen. His hand was long and bony. His voice . . ."

"But you refused?"

"I did."

Judith looked utterly exhausted. The faint flush of red about her cheeks had long since left her, and she was overwhelmed by a dry heaving motion. Matthew Beverley motioned to her father to assist her from the church, but as he put his arm around her shoulders she said loudly, "Last night a witch visited me."

A sudden silence fell.

"Last night, about the dead of the night, I felt a great weight upon my breast. When I awoke in the moonlight, I saw a likeness upon me which lay hold of my throat, and I had no strength or power in my hands to resist."

Matthew Beverley had moved to her side. "Tell us. Tell us the name of the witch."

She whispered something. He closed on her to hear what she said. "Don't be frightened. God knows all."

"God is my judge," Judith said, barely loud enough for a dozen or so to hear.

"Child, beware. To take his name in vain is blasphemy. Are you or are you not in league with the Devil?"

"No! No!" This time all heard her frantic denials.

The witch finder shook his head. "Then tell us this name, give us Satan's agent here in our midst." Turning violently and full upon the girl he roared, "Give us the witch's name."

Judith seemed tongue tied; Beverley seized her by the arms, holding her up. Bending his ear close to her lips, he hissed, "Speak, child. Name the imp of Satan."

Judith's head turned from side to side as if she were looking for a way of escape, but she was trapped. She whispered a name into Matthew Beverley's ear.

All eyes were fixed upon the witch finder. When he straightened his back, Beverley looked about him and demanded in a terrible voice. "Which of ye is Mistress Patience Cory?"

All eyes turned to Patience, but she didn't see them. The floor tilted, there was a roaring in her ears, and the room spun around her. Then darkness. Then silence.

"Going . . ."

"Going now . . ."

Hannah began to move restlessly in her chair; a moaning sound was forced from her lips. Dr. Marsh moved quickly to assert control.

"Hannah. I'm going to awaken you. Remember you must

wait for me to snap my fingers; then you may awaken. I am going to snap my fingers now."

She held her fingers close to Hannah's face and snapped them loudly. Hannah's moaning grew in intensity; her hands gripped the arms of the chair, her fingers making deep indentations in the fabric. She began rocking violently from side to side, nearly throwing herself to the ground in her agitation.

"Hannah." Dr. Marsh's voice cut through the moaning. "You will listen to my voice. When I snap my fingers you will awaken."

Almost imperceptibly the struggles began to subside. The fingers lost their tension, and Hannah became calm. Seizing her moment, Dr. Marsh said, "I am going to count down from five. At one you will open your eyes and feel rested. Five. Four. Three. Two." Again she snapped her fingers, this time close to Hannah's ear. "One."

Hannah's eyes opened.

"How do you feel?" asked Dr. Marsh.

"Tired."

"That will pass. Then you will have lots of energy. Do you remember anything?"

"I could hear your voice," she said softly. "But nothing else. I felt warm and comfortable and relaxed. Then after a while, I felt myself falling and there was a roaring in my ears. I was falling, but slowly, like a feather. I couldn't see anything, just a grayness and a feeling of being out of my body. I never felt asleep, though."

"That's a very common feeling," said Dr. Marsh. "And lots of patients say they were floating or falling. But did you remember any of my questions or your answers?"

148

"Something about school, I think," answered Hannah thoughtfully.

"Nothing more?"

"No."

"Does the name Patience Cory mean anything to you?"

Hannah's brow wrinkled. "I think I heard that name somewhere. Is it important? I just don't remember."

"You went into a trance."

"Did I do okay?"

"You did just fine," replied the doctor. "I'd like to think things through a little. Let's give it a break and meet in a week. Same time, same station. If anything happens, we'll get together sooner. You enjoy the rest of the day; it's beautiful out, and for once the humidity is low."

She walked Hannah to the end of the driveway. "Take care." Dr. Marsh watched her, a very puzzled look on her face, until she was out of sight.

12
Root Out Witches

THE NEXT MORNING HANNAH, AS USUAL, WENT jogging. During the first stages of her illness, she had been a compulsive exerciser. Now she enjoyed the freedom and solitude of a morning run.

She wondered what she had told Dr. Marsh under hypnosis. Probably all sorts of dumb things she had done as a child. She ran along Mrs. Chase's beach, continuing around the headland. At low tide there was a strip of firm, moist sand all the way to Menemsha.

There was a comfort in the mechanical nature of running. It required little thought, and after a while Hannah was able to switch her brain off and simply run by instinct. Now her morning jogging was in the nature of a habit, but a welcome one, and she was much looser about it than when she had first arrived at Stewart's Grove.

There wasn't much to do anyway. Greg was off to Am-

150

herst and would be away for several days. Several days! He didn't know how many. How could she live that long? What a week it had been. She had arrived a scared little girl not knowing anyone, dreading an indefinite exile on Martha's Vineyard, and now she had a boyfriend and two new friends in Keri and Steve. Just as important, she was feeling good, better than she had in two years. Still, several days. They would drag by. She had nothing to do until she went to the play with her aunt. Keri was busy working as a receptionist at the Harbor Inn during the days and rehearsing for *A Midsummer Night's Dream* in the evenings.

The weather turned hot, excessively so. Hannah spent the morning at Mrs. Chase's beach swimming and trying to get a suntan. She hadn't forgotten how pale she looked beside her friends.

In the afternoon, she explored the grounds of the estate. They were of far greater extent than she had expected. The woods, for example, covered several acres, and there was a maze of paths going through them.

Hannah felt a twinge of guilt; what should have been a perfect vacation—lying on the beach with no duties at all— had become boring. On Tuesday she discovered the branch library in West Tisbury. It had a pay phone, but whom could she call? Melanie couldn't take calls and Hannah's father would still be crisscrossing Egypt. She did take out several novels that were lighter in tone than those the butler had collected. In the past she had borrowed many books from the library at Reach Out and read them with great eagerness only to find out later that because of her illness or medicine she couldn't remember what they were about. In class they had read Shakespeare's *Tempest*, but she couldn't recall a word of it a month later. Now she found herself unable to concentrate on what she was reading because she kept seeing Greg's face and reliving the memory of their last kiss. Occasionally, too, she saw the look of burning jealousy on Arielle's face. Hannah wondered if she would have felt as Arielle did. She had to admit she would.

The day before she was to see *A Midsummer Night's Dream,* Mrs. Chase said to her at breakfast, "The Portuguese Festival is this afternoon." Mrs. Chase passed her the *Vineyard Gazette.* "There is a sizable Portuguese-American population in Oak Bluffs, and once a year they have a celebration and choose a queen. I'm going to Edgartown for my annual check-up, so I could drop you off. Mrs. Donohue will pick you up at five."

Hannah needed no second invitation; she was tired of her own company, and anything was better than lying about the beach covered in sunscreen.

"I'd love to go," Hannah replied, reading the article with interest.

When Mrs. Chase left her at Oak Bluffs the following afternoon, the heat was beginning to build. Hannah knew it was going to be an uncomfortable mix of a ninety-degree temperature and high humidity. Now more wise in the ways of island weather, she wore a pair of slip-on canvas sneakers, a white tank top edged in blue, and her light blue shorts. She tied her hair in a ponytail and wore the cap Keri had given her on *The Siren.*

The parade would not start until two o'clock, so she walked around the town. It was her first time in Oak Bluffs. The narrow main street was called Circuit Avenue, where she was astonished to find a massive wooden building containing, of all things, a huge carousel with handsome wooden horses prancing up and down to the accompaniment of a deafening calliope. As the platform spun faster and faster the horses rose and fell to the delighted shrieks of their tiny riders, most of whose faces were covered with pink and blue cotton candy.

At the top of a small hill was Trinity Methodist Church, surrounded by dozens of tiny cottages looking for all the world like the witch's house in "Hansel and Gretel." Each gingerbread house was surmounted by a high pitched roof and painted from a palette of pastel colors, its façade gaily festooned with gables, turrets, and scrollwork. Fleurs-de-lis and sunbursts like the paper lace used by bakeries filled every corner.

At two, Hannah joined the crowds thronging the sidewalk on Circuit Avenue. She sat on a bench with three children, all eating sandwiches. One of them had on a set of horn-rimmed glasses with thick lenses. "My name's Maria," she volunteered. "What's yours?"

"Hannah."

"Want one?" she asked, handing her a sandwich.

"What is it?" Hannah asked.

"Linguiça," Maria replied nonchalantly. "Sort of sausage."

"No, thank you," said Hannah, as politely as she could. The girl shrugged her shoulders.

The parade was short: in the lead was a police car; following on foot were four coast guard officers smartly dressed in uniform, and then the city officials.

A band followed with cheerleaders and baton twirlers, practically deafening the spectators with a Sousa march.

"My brother plays the trumpet," shouted Maria above the din. "He's bad."

Hannah smiled. Her new friend munched on her sandwich.

The center of the parade was reserved for the girl chosen to carry the crown of Queen Isabella.

153

"She fed the poor," Maria explained. "The girl's called Angelina. You Portuguese?"

"No. I'm not."

"Thought so. You don't know much," she said with satisfaction.

Angelina's blond hair was in a bun tucked up beneath a communion veil. Carrying the crown tightly in front of her, she was flanked by nine other girls dressed in white frilly dresses and matching patent-leather shoes. Tied to the crown and held by four of the communicants were four long red-and-white streamers twisting like corkscrews in the breeze.

Then it was over; the volunteer fire brigade rolled by with their engine's sirens going full blast. The crowd dispersed.

The sun was now at its hottest; Hannah decided to buy an ice cream. A year ago such a decision would have made her sweat with anxiety; now it seemed the natural thing to do.

A nearby restaurant advertised yogurt and soft ice cream in ten flavors. When Hannah opened the door, it was like walking into a refrigerator; she developed goose bumps.

The restaurant had a salad bar, and Hannah decided to eat a light lunch and then leave with an ice-cream cone.

Making a green salad, she surrounded it with tiny tomatoes and thin cucumber slices, smiling as she did so. Melanie hated "veggies," as she called them. Only the fear of gaining weight would drive her to eat salads, but nothing on earth would induce her to eat what she termed "the hard greens."

Hannah found a small table by the window, where she could see the people crossing Trinity Park and gazing at the densely packed filigree houses.

She wished her friend were with her, though when they went into a restaurant Melanie always commented on the other diners. If any boys were there, she wanted to flirt while

Hannah wished the ground would swallow her up. Usually there was no one who excited approval in Melanie. "Losers," she would say airily, casting a quick look around. "And two geeks."

Hannah had almost finished her salad when something made her look up. At first nothing seemed to have changed, but then, in a crowd of young people passing the window, she saw Greg.

She was about to tap on the window to attract his attention when an icy numbness came over her, freezing her hand in midair. Greg certainly didn't want to see her. Dressed in a T-shirt and khaki shorts, he was earnestly talking to a girl with a white sun visor shielding her eyes; his arm was around her shoulders. They both stopped and laughed at something he had said. He tweaked her visor, and she punched him playfully in the stomach. Then he pretended to be hurt and doubled up, just as he had done with her near Gay Head. The visitors parted on either side of him, a few people stopping curiously to see if he was all right.

A minute later the couple was swallowed up in the crowd.

Hannah sat motionless in her chair. Her anger and disappointment were crushing. The tightness in her chest made breathing difficult, but with an effort she pulled air into her lungs, and regained her composure. She placed her fork on the table slowly, feeling faint. Shutting her eyes, she bit down on her lower lip. Using the edge of the table for support and drawing herself upright, she walked unsteadily to the counter. Food had no attraction for her now. She paid for her salad.

"What about the ice cream, Miss?" asked the counterman. Then he saw the color of her face. "You okay?"

Hannah couldn't reply. There was a churning in her stomach, and tears running down her cheeks. She hurried into the bathroom. It was five minutes before her shoulders stopped heaving and she could splash cold water on her flushed face and pat it dry with a paper towel.

When she left the restaurant there was still a sick feeling in her stomach. Fifteen minutes ago she had been happy. Now she was miserable and hopeless.

Greg had a new girlfriend; someone who was everything she wasn't—pretty and lively and very self-confident. She hated the girl, she hated Greg, and worst of all, she hated herself. Greg had been nice to her because her aunt had asked him to be. He'd taken pity on a dumb teenager who had to see a shrink.

She'd misjudged him because she wanted to. He wasn't perfect. He resented the fact that the off-islander kids were rich. Yet that didn't stop him from going out in Steve's boat. He worked for the richest woman on the island. He'd made at least one disparaging remark about his grandparents, who looked after him all summer. He was proud of his scholarship, yet it was paid for by others.

When Mrs. Donohue picked her up in the Buick, she was sitting dejectedly on a bench. On the journey home, she responded to Mrs. Donohue's few questions with monosyllables.

At Stewart's Grove, Hannah hurried from the Buick to the luggage door. Inside, on the table, she was surprised to find a letter from Melanie. It had passed her own in the mail and was written in a very different tone from the exuberant one Melanie usually employed. Every word seemed to have been formed with an effort. Hannah's hands trembled as she read.

Dear Hannah,

I did something real dumb. After I wrote the last letter to you, things got real bad. I got in a row with Dr. Wilbanks, so I guess I won't be getting out of here soon. Remember how we talked about doing crazy things to ourselves? Well I was looking in the mirror and then, without thinking, I put my hands around my throat and squeezed. *I don't know why.* I quit in the end; the ringing in my ears stopped and everything was blurred.

I took a scarf from my drawer—that long red one—and went out to the trees at the back of the enclosed garden and wrapped it tightly around my neck and pulled as hard as I could. The first couple of times everything was soft and hazy and I fell down. Finally I got it to where I was cutting off air as well as the blood. But all that happened was my lungs would just about burst, and I had to let go.

When I came back in M. Desmoullins was there with his pimply girlfriend. Her name is Adèle, can you believe it? He asked me if I'd had a nice walk. And I said "Sure." I wanted to scream. I dropped French again.

I know it was dumb, and I don't want a lecture. Write me.

Love,
Melanie

Hannah realized she was crying. She went to the bathroom and got a glass of water and wiped her eyes on the towel. Then she found her stationery and a ballpoint and wrote.

Melanie,

Are you OK now? I miss you so much. Please don't do anything so foolish again. People love you. You have always been the strong one. It was you who told the musketeers to hold our ground against "The common crowds with bloody knives."

157

We all get depressed but we mustn't give in.

I'm sending this now. I've also got a weird dream to tell you about.

As soon as you get a week release I want you to stay here at Stewart's Grove.

Love you,

Hannah

P.S.   Write soon.

Hannah did not dare tell her about seeing Greg with his new girlfriend. Melanie couldn't handle any more bad news. She left the letter on the hall table as usual. For the rest of the day Hannah walked around the grounds of Stewart's Grove wishing she could call her friend.

In her room she pressed her forehead against the cool glass of the window. Tomorrow she would find out who the new girlfriend was, but she might never know why he preferred someone else. Could anything hurt so much? How could he have held her and kissed her and lied like that? At first it was humiliation she felt, but that emotion quickly turned to grief and regret. *In a few years,* Hannah thought sadly, *I'll look back on this and laugh at how silly I am.* She closed the drapes. No. Whatever happened, she wouldn't be laughing. It would always be too painful.

In bed, the tears brimmed in her eyes and slid down her cheeks. She started to cry, and once she'd begun she could not stop. The tears poured out, and every measure of control Hannah had managed to exert on the silent ride back from Oak Bluffs was lost. When she had cried herself out, she lay too exhausted to move or think.

Hannah slept uneasily before becoming aware of a constricting feeling in her throat. In the beginning it was hard to draw a breath. This she assumed was due to her weeping. However, she soon began to feel as if pressure were being increased around her neck. It was an enormous effort to suck breath into her tortured lungs. Her hands were trying to pry away an invisible cord that was cutting deep into her neck. She tried to scream but heard no sounds coming from her throat. Her body whipped back and forth. There was a terrible strain on her back muscles as she tried to lift herself from the bed. The room swirled around as the cord bit ever deeper and more fiercely into her flesh. A roaring grew inside her head like a thousand angry seas.

She tried to get out of bed, really tried. But her arms and legs were rubbery, and the rest of her felt like lead. "I will get up," she gasped, gritting her teeth, and by stubborn will alone, Hannah raised herself to a sitting position.

If she could have screamed, she would have. Instead, her body writhing and contorting, she fought with an unseen foe. Lights danced before her eyes. Above her the canopy of the bed was slowly descending.

Horror united with unbearable pain; slowly the canopy closed around her. Hannah thrashed her arms wildly, trying to draw a breath through a throat that was completely closed. She was being slowly suffocated.

The canopy of her bed seemed to envelop her. The room spun around her, turned red. Then black. Then nothing.

Ordeal

PATIENCE HAD SWOONED; THE HEAT AND EXCITE-
ment had been too much for her. Many thought, however,
that the accusations had struck home. Few would help raise
her up, but Jared did all he could for her, holding a cup of
water to her lips.

Beverley looked triumphant. "She must be close confined,"
he stated, "and carefully watched."

"Nonsense," Jared retorted. "She fainted in the heat and
why not?"

"Aye, 'tis nonsense," shouted William Cory, holding his
daughter as she sipped the water.

"She's a witch," Beverley continued. "She must be impris-
oned."

William Cory let forth a roar of anger. Seeing Patience
safe in Jared's arms, he got to his feet and lunged at the

160

witch finder, who hastily stepped back. "I'll show you witchcraft."

It took five men to prevent William Cory from reaching Matthew Beverley. They wrestled him to the ground, where he lay with his chest heaving. His face had become gray. "Help him home," Minister Slaughter said. "See he keeps to his bed."

Patience, with Jared's help, came to her father's side.

"Keep them apart," ordered Beverley, recovering his courage now William was no longer a threat.

Despite his daughter's protests, Cory was taken away. He continued to struggle, though he became weaker with every movement.

"'Tis for the best, child," Minister Slaughter told Patience. "No harm shall come to thee."

"She must be taken up and questioned," said Beverley. "Jailer, do your duty."

Giles Bailey, the constable and jailer, wanted to clasp irons on her there and then, but the minister refused to allow it, to the obvious displeasure of Matthew Beverley. As the girl was led away, Goody Perkins, surrounded as always by a brood of tattered children, declared loudly, "I always knew she was a witch, giving herself airs all the time."

Jared argued with the constable every inch of the way to the jail.

"Go home, Jared," said the constable. "The elders are bound to inquire more closely. If the girl is innocent, God will not let her suffer overmuch."

But it was not until Patience added her quiet pleadings that Jared would leave. Even so, he vowed to return the next morning even if "all the witches in Hell were loosed."

"Go help my father," Patience asked him. "His health has not been good of late. I shall not lack for company tonight."

The jail was a two-room wooden building set back from the main street. Patience had passed a thousand times without sparing it a glance. Now she quickened her pace as they passed the pillory, the whipping post, and the stocks.

Mr. Bailey thrust her roughly into the open cell. Most of those charged with witchcraft sat or lay here. There was Tribulation Wheatley, a poor dumb girl whose wits had long ago left her. Several others were notorious troublemakers, misfits and gossips—those the village could gladly spare. Patience recognized several against whom the most serious charges were leveled: Mary Leacock, Agnes Preston, Jennet Law, Susannah Swinton. Agnes lay on a cot, her clothes clinging damply to her body.

"What happened?" asked Patience, kneeling by her in the straw, but Agnes turned away to face the wall.

Jennet Law let out a cackle of laughter. "They swam her, child, and much good did it do them."

"Swam her?"

"Two days ago, secretly," she answered, "four men came and took her to Witch Pond. They tied her left thumb to her right great toe and her right thumb to her left toe. Then in she goes, clothes and all."

Now Patience understood. "For a witch will float."

"Yes, child, how well you've learned your lessons. And can ye say why?"

Patience could not.

"Water is for baptism; 'twill not receive anything impure," snapped Susannah Swinton from a corner of the room. "Now be silent, Jennet, and give us peace."

"And Agnes," continued Jennet, ignoring the interruption,

162

"did not sink but spun around like a heathen top. The water rejected her."

Patience recoiled from Agnes.

"Don't be alarmed, child," Jennet said, sitting beside Patience, her eyes glaring at her from beneath folds of skin. "Agnes's clothes held her up. A witch must be stripped to her shift. The fools didn't know that." She gave another cackle of laughter. "Had they left her two minutes her clothes would have filled with water, and she would have sunk like a stone. But then she would have been innocent." She paused and gently stroked Agnes's damp hair. "Innocent but drowned, poor lamb. You see, there's no way we can win. Once they make up their minds, we go like lambs to the sacrifice."

The door opened; the jailer's wife entered with trays containing bowls of soup and wooden spoons. Her husband followed with a loaf of black bread cut into pieces and several large pieces of cheese.

"We eat well here," commented Jennet. "We'll be fat enough for the hangman."

"Silence," commanded Mr. Bailey. "You're not here for your own pleasure. Patience, you must come with me. Fill your bowl and bring it with you."

Patience followed him as he led the way to a small inner cell beyond the first. It had an earthen floor and bars down one side. Behind the bars were chairs and seated in them were Matthew Beverley and Minister Slaughter.

"You shall be watched, child," said Minister Slaughter. "Master Beverley and I with the village elders will take turns."

Patience looked around the cell. There was no furniture, not even a stool. There was no window, but the rough boards let in chinks of light from the far wall. She had no appetite, so she stretched out on the heap of straw. Sleep soon overcame her, offering a respite from the day's sufferings.

Meals were forbidden her lest the devil should send a familiar spirit hidden in the bowl or trencher. She could not have eaten anyway; her stomach was contracted into one tight knot.

The watching continued into a second day, then a third. Patience could tell the passage of time by the narrow shafts of sunlight slanting through the ill-fitting boards.

She was allowed no visitors. Twice or thrice she heard Jared's voice protesting loudly as he sought entry, but the watchers were adamant. Some she knew well, and they were more kindly; but all were aware of the wiles of a witch, and they would not be drawn into talk with her, for the Devil was a great persuader. Only the minister, who urged her to prayer, and Matthew Beverley, who threatened her, dared to speak in her presence.

Patience quickly learned that the sound of the human voice, whatever the words, was most welcome. The hours dragged by, the watchers changed, becoming more frustrated as no imps appeared. Furthermore, they had to watch through the long nights while she slept the sleep of innocence.

"Do you deny you caused a pail to roll toward you," demanded Beverley on the fifth evening of watching, "as James Devers claims?"

"'Twas but a game."

"A game to bewitch a milking pail?"

Patience replied scornfully. "The child's words have been twisted. We merely set the pail on a hill and let it roll. He ran after it. What could be more innocent?"

"Take care, Mistress. If it should be found out that the pail ran uphill . . ."

"The pail will run uphill when a stream can be found to do so," Patience responded, with a courage she did not know she possessed.

"There are ways to make you confess," he said angrily. "Some have been tormented with red-hot pincers, some flayed alive. None can resist the rack. You will not be so pert when the pain starts."

"If I am a witch, as you claim, will I not be able to stand pain?" replied Patience, settling down in the straw.

"If? There is no 'if' about it. I will see you hanged before I leave this village, and think it shame that burning is not practiced. 'Tis pity that in old and New England witchcraft is a mere felony instead of heresy, but within the month I shall see your witch's corpse dangling from a rope, Mistress Cory." Then he sank heavily into his chair.

Patience felt the goose bumps on her arms but was determined to show no fear. At midnight she awoke; there was someone outside the cell door. It opened, and there stood Matthew Beverley, Minister Slaughter, and two women. "You must be searched, Mistress," said the witch finder.

Patience ran to the far corner of the cell. "No," she gasped. "I will not."

"Patience, it's for your own protection," said the minister. "If you refuse, we must assist the women. It is better for all. . . ." The men left with the two watchers.

"Come, Mistress," said Goodwife Bailey. "We must make an examination."

"Examination," gasped Patience, "for what?"

The other woman was the wife of Deacon Merriweather, a shrew, forever sticking her long nose into the business of

165

others. Her voice was high pitched and whiny. "Remove your garments," she commanded.

Patience still could not comprehend her meaning. "But why?"

Goodwife Bailey began pulling at Patience's dress. "You must be searched inch by inch to see if you have a secret teat from which Satan or your familiar spirits may suckle."

"Please," begged Patience, "do not do this. . . ."

"If you are innocent, you have nothing to fear," said the deacon's wife. "Shall we call for the men to assist us?"

She had hoped they would not demand the removal of her shift, but in vain.

"Does the shift hide your sin?" demanded Mrs. Merriweather. "Off with it!"

Naked she stood before them. They poked and pried into every part of her until, at last, they confessed disappointment. There was no secret teat to suckle imps. Patience was allowed to dress.

Matthew Beverley was furious when he was told. "Bind her," he commanded, as Patience stood before him. "And tightly too."

"Now, brother," Minister Slaughter began, "surely 'tis not—"

"She shall be bound. Bound I say."

A heavy oak chair was brought in, and the jailer, who had lost much of his earlier enthusiasm, tied Patience's hands and feet to it. "She is to be kept sleepless and without food," the witch finder commanded, "and a small hole must be cut in the wall to allow her imps to come to her. They who watch must be ever and anon sweeping the room, and if they see any spiders or flies that they cannot kill, those are imps of Satan."

166

All night she sat. The minutes crept by on leaden feet. The feeling left her feet and hands. The numbness crept slowly throughout her body. After ten hours Patience thought she heard noises in the cell, but no one was moving or speaking. Then she felt a dull roaring in her ears and the floor began to tilt first one way then the other. Though seated, she could not keep her balance and toppled first to one side of the chair, then the other. The roaring in her head grew in volume.

Minister Slaughter grew alarmed. Matthew Beverley was summoned. "'Tis more devilment," he proclaimed. "Leave her be."

But the minister would not heed him. Patience was untied and carried to the straw at one end of the cell. By vigorous rubbing of her legs and arms, the watchers restored feeling to the limbs. Then it was as if a thousand pins had been stuck in her limbs. Patience wept in pain and frustration.

"She cannot be tied for more than one hour at a time," declared the Reverend Slaughter. "She is to be permitted to walk around her cell ten times at every hour."

"Monstrous!" exclaimed the witch finder. "Unless she suffers, her devilish master and his imps will not succor her. I have known cases—"

"Enough," the minister commanded with a determination he had not shown before. "It shall be as I say." And with that Beverley had to be satisfied. He left the jail in ill humor.

The next night, a brown rat was seen by Henry Makepeace, watcher. Despite all attempts the creature could not be caught—certain proof of its diabolical nature. A triumphant Matthew Beverley was paid his fee. He had trapped a witch. Now he could help condemn one. Minister Slaughter sent a full report to the authorities in Boston and a trial was ordered forthwith.

* * *

It was a very different Patience Cory who was brought to the meetinghouse for her trial two weeks later. Her hair had lost all its luster, and her bright eyes were dulled from lack of sleep. She dragged her feet, for when she had been bound the blood had collected in her feet.

The room was packed; already the heat was barely tolerable. Around her Patience at first saw only a blur of faces, and when she appeared, fully half the children present began to wail and to scream at her. The noise was deafening.

Judge Josiah Grimsted had been sent from Boston. His look was stern, though he had a reputation for fairness. His great black hat rested on the table in front of him, and he wore a large, full-bottomed white wig. He was the only man present not dressed in black. Had it not been for his exalted position there would certainly have been comment about his bottle-green coat. Before him stood a large pewter inkstand near a stack of parchment and several freshly sharpened quill pens. He had a gavel. On his right sat Minister Slaughter and on his left, Matthew Beverley. At either end of the table were two church elders. In vain did Patience seek out a face with a glimmer of mercy or compassion. All looked grave, some hostile. This was her jury.

"Silence," roared the judge. "Silence or all of you shall be fined. This is no theater." The noise subsided; many of the children eyed Patience, nudged each other, and pointed.

Jared assisted Patience to a chair placed before the judges. "Your father is well and sends his love," he whispered.

"What ails these afflicted children?" the magistrate asked Patience.

She tried to lick her swollen lips. When she spoke nothing

could be heard. Jared poured her a cup of water. She drank gratefully.

"Pray, Mistress Cory, tell me what ails these affrighted children?"

"I do not know." The words were little more than a series of dry raspings.

"What do you think disturbs them?"

She gave no response.

"Do you think they are bewitched?"

"No."

"They appear bewitched to me," said the judge.

Angered and frightened, Patience turned on the children. "What have I done to you? Do you not know God sees through your tricks?"

"We do God's bidding," said little Polly Dawson primly.

"We are his instruments," added Deliverance Seaton solemnly.

"I have done you no wrong," Patience answered. "Did I not nurse you, Polly, when you had the fever? If anyone is in the Devil's power, it is these poor demented children, not I. And you, Deliverance Seaton, do not even know the meaning of the word 'instrument.'"

The children backed away and resumed their wailing and pointing. "How comes it that your appearance seems to frighten them so?" asked Matthew Beverley, triumphantly.

"They hurt themselves. I do not harm them."

The children broke into screaming and wailing. One ran to her and pointed to her shoulder, crying. "She has little birds on her shoulder, one green, one red. She showed me these birds one morning after sunup." At this the children began a fresh chorus of lamentation.

Judge Grimsted again demanded silence; it was restored with difficulty.

"She must be held," Minister Slaughter insisted, "or she may bewitch all of us."

"Aye, I suppose you must stand," the judge said with little enthusiasm, and at his nod the minister appointed Matthew Greenfield and Silas Turner to hold Patience's hands. "This way you cannot clench your fists to pinch the afflicted. And you must fix your eyes on us and not look on these children or anyone else, for they cry out when your eye falls upon them. Jared Cheever, see you keep your distance," he added, seeing the young man approaching the prisoner.

"She cannot stand," Jared protested. "Let her father support her if I may not."

William Cory, with a grateful look at Jared, hastened to his daughter's side.

"We will have no more interruptions," the judge declared. "And let me also say great caution must be exercised in the matter. Legality is very important."

"Legality," snapped Patience's father. "There has yet to be an accusation that makes any sense. Is the law of Massachusetts now dependent on the words of half a dozen children who need more of the rod and less—"

"You will be silent," the judge ordered, "or you shall be put out." He leaned forward and ruffled through a stack of papers before him before selecting one. "It is too easy to put words into the witch's mouth. The only confessions of merit are those freely offered. A witch must freely declare she be a witch. Let Judith McKay come forward."

Judith stepped to the front of the room and faced the judges. In her right hand she took a Bible and swore to tell the truth. Then she kissed the book and laid it on the judges' table.

She gave her testimony calmly, but those at the back of the hall had difficulty hearing.

"Last year on Martinmas Eve, I passed Patience Cory on the road to Chilmark village. She spoke to me and looked strangely at me. That night I dreamed of a thing like an Indian all dark with black hair." There was a gasp from the villagers. "He told me I must serve him for seven years. He had a book."

"What was in the book?" asked the judge.

"Writing."

"Can you read?"

Judith looked embarrassed. "It was devilish writing," she said lamely.

"She dreamed this foolishness," said Jared. "She cannot read. Judith, end this foolishness. Are all books you cannot read the handwork of the Devil?"

"Silence!" Judge Grimsted interrupted him. "You will have an opportunity to speak."

Flashing a look of pure hatred at Jared, Judith added, "In the book I saw names written in blood. Agnes Preston, Patience Cory, and others. I know names when I see them."

"Nonsense," said Jared. "Agnes Preston can barely make her mark; she knows nothing of writing."

"The Devil taught her," snapped Matthew Beverley. "He writes a broad hand."

"And Jennet Law has a cat that becomes an owl," continued Judith.

The judge raised his hand. "We are here to inquire of Patience Cory, not of any others. They are not yet on trial."

One by one, accusers came forward and told their stories. Hour after hour they droned on. Widow Bishop had met a raccoon that arched its body and spit fire at her. Susan Tayleure's child had complained of pins being stuck into him.

By afternoon, Patience was allowed to rest in a chair, her hands no longer held, for it was clear she had no strength left. Yet even in this condition she had thought for others. "Father, you look pale," she said softly during a momentary lull in the trial. "Is it your chest?"

"'Tis nothing, child, just the heat, that's all."

The evidence continued. Many spoke on behalf of Patience, describing her as one of the most kindly and generous persons on the island. But whenever they did, the children set up such a caterwauling that Patience's chances were hurt rather than helped. When some of the villagers found they were likely to be accused by the afflicted ones, they chose to hold their tongues.

The hours passed slowly. The hard edge of Patience's chair bit into her thigh; when she moved her weight, another pain began. Twice, in spite of everything, her eyes closed and her head dropped, and twice she was awakened, for the magistrate felt the trial should be, above all things, just.

The time came for William Cory to speak on behalf of his daughter.

"My daughter is no more a witch than you or I," he began, looking directly at Matthew Beverley, who gnawed his bottom lip in fury. "All we have heard is rubbish, a few facts given fantastical twists by foolish children."

The afflicted children began to moan at this, and Deliverance Seaton fell to her knees in the aisle, making the most piteous sounds.

172

"It is fantastical," continued Patience's father. "And these children are no more bewitched than my cow, Buttercup."

Several people scoffed at him, but when his eye fell upon them, they became silent.

"You offer no proof," snapped Matthew Beverley. "Assertion is not proof."

"And this is proof?" demanded William Cory, throwing his hands up in disgust. "Silly old wives' tales, childish nonsense."

"Do you deny the existence of witches?" cried Beverley, leaping to his feet and slapping his hand against the table.

"I say this. I see none on trial. If any here be witches, let them strike me down. I defy them, and I defy the Devil himself."

A shocked silence fell; William Cory was deliberately taking his life into his own hands. It was a foolhardiness never before seen in this meetinghouse. Matthew Beverley sat back in his chair, for once speechless.

The silence continued; no one dared move for fear of attracting the wrath that was sure to follow. The afflicted children seemed confused.

"So," concluded William, "it seems Satan and his witches are powerless here."

At this there were murmurs of agreement. Patience had never loved her father so much. Jared shook William's hand.

The witch finder came out of his trance, his face purple with rage. "Do you deny the power of this court to find out the truth?"

"This court has served Satan's purpose well," answered William Cory, sensing victory. "Neighbor fights with neighbor, the . . . the—" He broke off, appearing to have difficulty in catching his breath. "The innocent are condemned though they deny their guilt before God."

Matthew Beverley seized his chance. "A witch will not confess to being a witch, that much is clear."

"And so everyone who claims to be innocent is guilty?"

That argument hit home with many of those present; loud murmurings of assent rose from the benches.

Deliverance Seaton, unseen by most, had been slowly walking down the aisle toward William Cory, her finger pointing at him. As she drew near, all eyes turned to follow her progress until she stood before William Cory.

In a thin high-pitched voice, Deliverance said, "I see him."

"Whom do you see, child?" demanded Matthew Beverley. "Tell us."

"Satan."

There was an instinctive recoiling on everyone's part. Even William Cory seemed unnerved by the child's quiet assurance. He passed a hand over his eyes. Patience thought he looked as old and ill as he had on the endless nights he had vainly prayed by his dying wife's bedside. Licking dry lips, he spoke. "Where do you see Satan?"

The child's finger pointed directly at William's shoulder. The angelic little face was suddenly filled with hatred. "He sits on your shoulder, in the form of a tiny red bird with long white tail feathers. It is Satan." She spit out the words venomously. "And he sits on your shoulder."

William Cory's hands clutched at his heart. Then he straightened his body, took a deep breath, and spoke with a voice full of emotion yet under control. "I tell this court that this procedure is a defilement of all God's law and justice. Are we to listen to the babblings of children—"

174

Judge Grimsted rapped sharply on the table with his gavel. "You must be silent."

"I will not be silenced. Are we so . . . are we so . . ."

From William Cory's mouth came the gurgling sounds of a man who would speak but was prevented by forces beyond his own. Two steps forward he took, then a third. Finally he fell, the judges' table crashing over with him.

Deliverance Seaton, on her lips a smile as beautiful as only a child could form, looked down at the writhing body of William Cory, and in the shocked silence that followed William Cory's collapse, said sweetly, "The bird flew away."

Pandemonium broke out; William Cory was borne home on a hurdle, a leech ministering to him. Jared was torn between his desire to go with William and his love for Patience.

At last, when a semblance of order was restored, Judge Grimsted ordered a recess until the following day. Jared was permitted to wipe the tears from Patience's eyes and the sweat from her weary face. Only Beverley opposed the break in Patience's examination, growling, "She was hale enough when it came to tormenting people; she is strong enough to be questioned."

The judge silenced him. "Let Mistress Cory be taken back to the jail. She may sleep. Tomorrow Jared Cheever will speak in her defense. We shall all pray for the health of William Cory."

Minister Slaughter led them in prayer and spoke the benediction.

14
Midsummer Nightmare

HANNAH AWOKE WITH A START, SITTING UP IN bed, the dream still running through her mind. It was as clear as a television play. And there could no longer be any doubt about it: Patience was trying to communicate with her. She remembered Dr. Marsh asking her if she had heard the name Patience Cory. But she had no answers, only questions. What had she said while she'd been hypnotized? What did events of so long ago have to do with her? Was there some connection between Patience's story and her own life? How could there be?

Hannah had never been to Martha's Vineyard before, and she had never heard of Patience Cory. As for witches, she knew only what she'd read about them in school.

She was determined to put the dream behind her, frightening though it had been. One thing for sure, she was not going to be overwhelmed by nightmares. She must put her desolation and despair behind her and get on with her life.

When she set out from the luggage door, it was only six o'clock, and the air still had the scent of dawn about it. The sky remained mysterious, not yet ready to tell what kind of day it was to be.

The dew moistened her Nikes as she jogged toward the cliff path. Mist still obscured the horizon, though she could just pick out the bobbing row of buoys and flags that marked off Mrs. Chase's beach; beyond them the sea was empty and cheerless. In the distance foghorns sounded a melancholy chorus. *Yoo-hoo, yoo-hoo.*

It was over with Greg. Her mother's death had already taught her this kind of bitter lesson. Love meant losing, and joy meant pain. But it didn't have to be the end of the world. She didn't have to starve herself to death. No, she was past that stage. Life would go on. Hannah Kincaid would get over this even though she couldn't imagine how. Without any purpose, she found herself jogging north toward the greenhouses beyond Stewart's Grove.

"Miss Hannah," said a voice from inside the doorway of one of them. "You're up early."

Mr. Donohue, his hat flattened on his head, was smiling at her.

"So are you. I couldn't sleep."

"Come on in here. Have a cup of coffee."

At one end of the greenhouse he had a Mr. Coffee pot and several large mugs. "I have some of that cream stuff," he said, "and sugar somewhere." He waited while she caught her breath.

Hannah accepted a cup with eagerness, holding it between

her hands for warmth before setting it down and pouring in the cream and a packet of sugar.

"Everyone my age drinks it black," he commented, "usually without sugar. I couldn't drink it that way, not even in the war. Second World War, I mean. Been a few since then, but nothing like the big one. I was twenty-four when I got my draft notice. Wasn't doing much, so I thought it would be exciting. I'd never traveled, you see. Born and bred in Hudson . . . miles from anywhere."

His eyes had a faraway look; Hannah felt she should say something but wasn't sure what.

The coffee tasted bitter; Hannah still hadn't gotten used to coffee, but wasn't hot chocolate just for kids?

"Were you in the army?"

"Yes." He eyed her shrewdly. "I served in North Africa and Italy. Blood-and-Guts Patton was our general. Anyway, one morning I couldn't get out of bed. Nerves went, you see. Thank god the general never heard about it. After that I wasn't much use for anything, so I became a gardener and handyman. I like plants more than most people. No evil in them, I guess."

He stopped and picked up his pipe, which lay on a pile of wooden flats. "Don't say this much usually. Not a great talker, me."

From his inside pocket he took a tobacco pouch and filled his pipe. "You see, Miss Hannah, there's some of us feels more than most. I could sense you'd suffered when I first met you."

Tearing a match from a pack, he struck it and held it over the bowl of the pipe. He sucked the flame down, and soon the tobacco glowed red. "And sometimes, most times, that's not good. There's a lot of pain that others don't feel." He sat on an upturned wheelbarrow, Hannah opposite on a pile of bricks. "I reckon you think about things too much. Perhaps you're looking for something that isn't possible." He pulled on his pipe. "I thought death would be beautiful, like some kind of cloud of forgetfulness. I said to myself, When I die there'll be some great revelation, everything will fit together. I thought all this lying in bed those many years ago."

"And what happened?"

"I was recuperating in England." Taking the pipe from his mouth, he showed her the bowl, which was carved in the shape of a bulldog. "Got this pipe there. England is a beautiful country, best gardens in the world. The hospital was one of those great mansions belonging to some lord. When I felt better I used to go for walks, sort of like you're doing now. One day I met this man. He had a beard and a wonderful kindly smile. We got to talking, and he told me lots of people felt the same way I did. You know, expecting things to be just so. It was strange, meeting him like that. I'd never seen him before, and I never did again. He said, 'Come with me, I want to show you something in my greenhouse.' It must have been his house and gardens." Pulling on his pipe, the gardener seemed lost in thought. Hannah sipped her coffee until she could bear the suspense no longer.

"What did he show you?"

Mr. Donohue got up and motioned to her to accompany him. Halfway down the greenhouse he stopped. "This is what he showed me."

They were surrounded by flowers, deep borders of delphinium, lupine, and campanula bells, mounds of Shasta daisies with huge white flowers. Beyond stood lilies of every alluring shade and color, some pale enough to be almost white, others dark as purple plums, with lime-yellow throats.

Gazing at them with undisguised delight, he added softly, "I never felt that depressed again."

"They are beautiful," said Hannah, knowing no words could do justice to the scene before her.

Mr. Donohue took his pipe from his mouth and looked at her closely before saying, "I reckon you've seen her by now, haven't you?"

Hannah looked at him, puzzled. "Seen who?"

"Why, the little Puritan girl. I figured she was a ghost, but when I told people, they thought I was crazy. So I shut up."

"You've seen her too?" she asked the gardener.

"Lots o' times. She wanted something, but I never could figure out what. She used to lead me to the old bakehouse."

"I saw her in Long Walk. I thought it was a dream."

"So did I at first, but it weren't. Only certain people can see her, I guess. Keep it to yourself, Miss Hannah, unless you want people looking at you funny. Well, I've said more than I thought to. Good day, Miss Hannah."

And before she could ask him any questions, he raised his battered hat to her and went back to his beloved flowers.

When Mrs. Donohue returned with the mail, Hannah was apprehensive to find an envelope in Melanie's handwriting. Its contents soon put her fears to rest.

Booby Hatch

July something

Dear Hannah,

Oh God I'm feeling so much better. Forget that crazy letter I sent.

Guess what! I've found one! A real, genuine, honest-to-goodness boyfriend. No zits, great lips.

I got my first mid-week pass, and I went with Susan Friedly and a bunch of others. I had on my red top and my black stretch pants. I looked *sexy*. The chaperone was Anna Buckowski, you know, El Blimpo. How can somebody be six feet tall *and* fat? When we got to the disco place, 'Bright Lights and Promises,' a peculiar feeling came over me. This guy was giving me the eye. Blond and blue-eyed. His muscles rippling under his Hard Rock Cafe sweatshirt (the black one). And could he dance? My dear, I was quite breathless. It was *Dirty Dancing* all over again.

I thought he was with some bimbette, a thin creature in a knee-length skirt and tacky bleached hair BUT NOOOO! She was with his friend.

And when he asked me to dance—Oh joy that is in our embers! His strong suntanned arm around my slim waist. The electricity coursed through me. The impact of the flashing lights and ear-shattering music. The kaleidoscope of colors. He is at least three inches taller than me, which is perfect.

Oh my dear, it was a night to remember. The last dance is the slow one, and I'll swear I could feel the beating of his heart. And then HE KISSED ME! I was so surprised, I forgot to close my eyes. Twice more he kissed me. I went positively gaga! And I know *I* got it right.

Well to cut a long story short, as someone once said, we agreed to meet the following week. I didn't tell him about the Booby Hatch. His name is Chris, and he's GOR-GEE-US! But much more important was knowing he was interested in ME!

Dr. Wilbanks says he's pleased with me. You will be thrilled to hear I am 'no longer sacrificing contact with reality.' I know there are things we can't control. My mom did what she did, and it wasn't my fault.

What's all this stuff about ghosts? You're kidding, right? How come little ol' you is following lights down dark passages? You must be cured.

Mrs. Pascoe caught the flu, so the inventory is delayed. YOUR NAME came up as a felon. I don't know what the book was yet, but when I do, I'll slip in a new old card!

Love ya,
M

PS. Later.

Melanie's letter was so upbeat that Hannah tried to answer in the same vein.

July 19

Dear Melanie,

I got your letter today about Chris. I'm so happy for you. Greg has been away for a while so there are no new developments to report.

We did go watch the fireworks on Steve's boat. It was fun.

Hannah looked at what she had written, then tore it up in disgust. She couldn't get any warmth or enthusiasm into her reply. It was better to delay a response until she felt better about Greg. How could she tell her best friend, who was so happy, that Greg was dating another girl? Oh, why did he have to lie to her?

To be fair, she wasn't his girlfriend; they had never had a date alone. He'd kissed her, but that wasn't any kind of promise. And the more she thought about it, the more she realized how silly she was being. It was the constant doubting of her worth or value that had helped put her in Reach Out in the first place. When she'd begun to feel good about herself again—and it hadn't happened overnight—she'd been ready to leave.

Common sense told Hannah she would have many boyfriends; at fifteen she wasn't thinking of marriage. Still, it had hurt more than she'd thought possible to see Greg with another girl. And it was too soon to write to Melanie about it.

In the narrow bathroom she gazed critically at the face in the mirror. It was flushed, and her eyes looked puffy. Tea bags soaked in water would bring the swelling down, but she didn't feel like asking Mrs. Donohue and facing the inevitable questions. She splashed cold water on her eyelids, and some of the puffiness disappeared.

Her hair was as troublesome as ever. She washed it and added a conditioner to make it shine. Then she fashioned a tiny side braid, trimming off two stray wisps with her manicure scissors. When it was dry, Hannah put on a coral lip gloss and applied a light dusting of blush high on the cheekbones as Melanie had taught her.

Hannah wore her one designer dress, the bright blue print with tiered bottom by Jessica McClintock, and chose a pair of flat-soled black shoes, which she figured would be best for the outdoor theater.

Her aunt nodded approvingly. "I'm glad you aren't wearing high heels. We do have to walk some distance across a field."

Mrs. Chase drove the Cadillac with skill and care, avoiding rough patches whenever possible. She never went above forty miles an hour.

The restaurant, Le Chateau, was set in an art gallery. There was an indoor terrace with a fountain at its center, but Mrs. Chase preferred to sit outside in the garden, surrounded by flowers and the cool green of beautiful plantings. Hannah was a little nervous. She had horrible visions of knocking over a glass of water or picking up the wrong fork.

She looked at the menu in bewilderment. The choices were endless and all in French. Her two years of study were totally inadequate. *Veau gigot?* What was *caille* or *homard?* Why hadn't she listened more closely to Monsieur Eschenazy? How could she ever expect to be sophisticated when she was always out of her depth?

"You must try the lobster with cognac cream sauce," Mrs. Chase said from behind the huge menu. "Perhaps you would like me to order for you."

Hannah was happy to let her great-aunt take charge. Mrs. Chase addressed the waiter fluently in French.

It was a most elegant restaurant; already one couple in shorts had been turned away.

"I've selected the quail with grapes and raspberries," Mrs. Chase said, looking around the terrace with its blue and coral linens and candle-lit tables. "My dear husband always liked Le Chateau. He understood so much about wines."

Hannah was determined not to spoil things for her aunt. She ate everything and praised everything. Conversation lagged occasionally, but her aunt did not notice. Fortunately, the portions were small, but it was more food than she had eaten at one sitting for as long as she could remember. Her aunt looked very pleased. At least she's happy, thought Hannah. I haven't ruined her treat.

Just as they were leaving, a man came over to them. Mrs. Chase blushed. Hannah couldn't believe her eyes. The two adults talked eagerly out of her hearing, and when they parted, her aunt said nothing to Hannah by way of explanation.

Her aunt drove along State Road saying nothing until they

joined the line of vehicles passing between two stone pillars at the entrance to the outdoor arena.

"My husband donated this land to the Vineyard Players," Mrs. Chase said as they pulled into the parking lot. "The rest of it he sold to the Tisbury Waterworks—on condition they supported the summer performances. He was always careful to get his money's worth. I get complimentary tickets, but I never use them. The arts are always short of money."

She paid for their tickets, and they followed the woodland path down the hill to the open-air theater. As they walked among the trees, they could hear music coming from all around them. Sometimes it was in the branches above; at others it came from beds of flowers.

The performance took place in a natural amphitheater, almost a leafy cathedral. A flat, grassy area formed the stage; a gentle slope dominated at the top by a giant white oak served as the auditorium. Some people sat on the cool, grassy carpet, but Mrs. Chase and Hannah had folding chairs in the front row.

Hypolita got a round of applause for her costume alone, a tight leopard skin, but Keri was undoubtedly the best actor. When she chased Demetrius into the wood, clutching at him and saying, "I am your spaniel, and the more you beat me, I will fawn on you," Hannah felt a tear roll down her cheek.

Still, the play was a comedy. Bottom kept everybody laughing, and the best part was the way the actors moved through the audience, entering and exiting in different places and even bringing some of the spectators into the action.

Hannah, however, found herself thinking about Greg. He was exactly what she wanted in a man. She could still feel his lips on hers and see his smile. And now he was dating another girl and probably kissing *her*. Maybe they were dancing together. Would he smile at her the same way he had at Hannah? She mustn't think about him. He wasn't the only guy in the world.

Resolutely she turned her attention back to the antics of Bottom and the fairies.

After the play the actors mingled with the spectators. Steve was there. He was in charge of properties, and his biggest concern was guarding the papier-mâché head that transformed Bottom the weaver into a donkey. Everyone wanted to try it on, much to his alarm.

In the excitement no one mentioned Greg to Hannah, and she was thankful.

Mrs. Chase said nothing as they left the parking lot and followed the stream of cars along State Road. Soon they turned off onto North Road, leaving the other traffic as it headed down-island. The seats in the Cadillac were deep and plush. Hannah yawned. She felt very tired, and she was so comfortable. She felt herself floating, floating. . . .

Verdict

NOT ONE MOMENT OF SLEEP DID PATIENCE HAVE that night. Her father's life was despaired of, though he rested comfortably, with Jared by his side. Patience had asked him to remain with her father, for he could do nought for her. William Cory would never be the man he used to be, but that was kept from her. Judge Grimsted ordered the trial to go forth, over the protests of many right-thinking men and women.

No sooner had Patience entered the meetinghouse than the children created an uproar. Polly Dawson and Deliverance Seaton immediately fell to the floor with howls of pain, clutching their stomachs. At least half a dozen began shrieking, "a red bird, a red bird," and pointing to the rafters.

It was fully ten minutes before order was restored. Judge Grimsted announced that he would brook no more outbursts. His tone left no question he meant it. "Any child who speaks out of turn will be sent from the court and lodged in the jail until this trial is over," he said fiercely. "And I caution their parents. Any disturbance from their child, and they shall be fined."

The room was quiet. The judge signaled Jared to speak. Standing at the side of the room where he could turn easily from jury to villagers, Jared was but two paces from Patience.

"The Devil," he began, "cannot change from a spirit to mortal flesh unless God himself commands it. Satan cannot assume a bodily form. The Devil is not flesh but spirit; he cannot appear as a man with a book."

This reasoning impressed many, Minister Slaughter among them. He turned to Beverley and said, "How answer you that, brother?"

Thinking furiously, Beverley got to his feet, his chair scraping against the pine floorboards. "I say to this young man there be a hundred, a thousand, confessions of witches. How can they all be innocent?" Sitting down, he was gratified to hear murmurs of assent.

"I know nothing of confessions," Jared responded. "All of us know how easy it is to sin, and most have a sense of guilt. 'Tis an easy thing for this guilt to be taken for more than it is by the overly credulous."

"We do not understand everything," the minister said in agitation. "Young man, do not attempt to explain all things by reason. *Non est religio ubi omnia patent.* Where there is no mystery, there is no religion."

"The ways of God remain a mystery," Jared conceded, "but those of jealous, spiteful women do not. Patience is accused of having little birds on her shoulder."

"A sure sign," the witch hunter claimed. "Agents of Satan."

"The child saw them after sunup. Does a witch's familiar not vanish before sunrise? Yea, long before, for the Devil and his agents must be gone by cockcrow."

Matthew Beverley was silent. All eyes turned to him. He tried to speak but appeared confused by this argument. Finally he hesitantly replied. "The Devil has the power to stop roosters from crowing. The birds went back to Hell, then the cocks crew." Looking around, he was aware of the weakness of his argument. Several who had supported him before looked doubtful. There was some embarrassed coughing from the benches. Then silence.

Jared continued in a quiet, firm tone. "All the testimony, so called, we have heard is based upon events that have a natural explanation or upon the words of children. No one laid blame upon Patience before. Why now is she condemned? Because a man is sick, because another is jilted, because a cow stops giving milk, must Patience Cory be the cause? Was no one sick in this village before? Cows have stopped giving milk in Chilmark and Tisbury before Patience was born." He looked around the room, encouraged to find some heads nodding in agreement. "Before anyone in this room was born." There he paused to let his argument take hold.

The judge appeared genuinely perplexed. "We must decide what is truth and where it lies. There is no doubt much imposture is practiced where witchcraft is concerned. Was Mistress Cory searched?"

"Aye, she was," replied the minister. "But naught was discovered."

"No warts, no teats?"

"None."

"She was not searched by those skilled in it," Beverley said angrily.

"Was she watched?"

"Aye," said Beverley, "and an imp appeared in the form of a rat, did it not, Minister Slaughter?"

"There was a rat," agreed the minister, shifting uncomfortably in his chair. "But as to it being a . . ."

"You saw a rat," said Jared, his voice heavy with sarcasm. "Who here has been so unlucky as to see an imp disguised as a rat? No doubt the prisoners do get a ration of cheese."

For the first time that day, there was laughter. Beverley turned bright red, from either confusion or rage. "Had we caught the creature, we would have had the proof of witchcraft."

"The rat went back to Hell," added Jared. "Did it not?"

"It did," affirmed the witch finder, falling into the trap. This time laughter swept around the meetinghouse. Patience looked up and managed a weak smile, despite her peril and exhaustion.

Joshua McKay, father of Judith, strode angrily to the front of the room. "Ye think it amusing that my daughter is bewitched, do ye? Well, 'tis no laughing matter for the child or her mother and me." He glared at Jared. "And I think it shame that a man who spoke to her of love should now abuse her. Well, Jared, what did Judith do to you, that you scorn her?"

Jared looked at the floor. "I cannot say; 'tis up to Judith."

Judith stood slowly. "I lost his love because I was bewitched by Patience Cory. She made potions and gave them to him."

"And where are these potions?" asked the judge.

"I cannot find them," she confessed. "But one day spectral

190

powder was thrown into my eyes and people witnessed it there. I was blinded for a day."

"Which people?" demanded the judge. "Let them come forward." No one rose to affirm Judith's claim.

Polly Dawson was called, a child of six years. She claimed Patience had looked queerly at her while pretending to help her through the snow. That night, her mother claimed, she was strangely distorted in her joints and thrown into such convulsions as astonished spectators. In addition she was cruelly pinched with invisible hands. Black-and-blue marks were visible though they disappeared immediately. This too happened about Martinmas.

"Did you tell your mother everything?" asked Jared.

The little girl nodded.

"Have you seen any witches on broomsticks?"

"Oh, yes," said Polly.

"And a black man with colored birds on his shoulder?"

Again the girl nodded.

"And have you seen the witches dancing late at night?"

"Oh, yes."

"Were people here dancing with them?"

"Yes, many."

"Mistress Cory?"

"Yes."

"Me?"

"Yes."

Jared pointed to the judge. "Him?"

"Yes."

"And the man next to him with the beard?"

"Yes."

"Enough," cried Judge Grimsted, in irritation. "This child agrees with anything she is asked. Her parents are much at

191

fault. I charge you, Minister Slaughter, to see she is catechized thoroughly." Then he dismissed the child with a wave of his hand. "Let us have no more such nonsense."

The morning session finished. Patience, almost in a stupor, heard the noise of chairs scraping across the floor. The chattering of the spectators, so unusual in the meetinghouse, finally convinced her a recess had been called.

She was not taken back to the jail; the constable guarded her but ordered Jared to bring her a cool drink of water; he also brought a blueberry muffin, but she shook her head at it.

After the noon recess, more witnesses were called and examined. Jared showed many to be addled in their wits and the rest to be envious or plain malicious.

In vain, Matthew Beverley demanded his silencing. The judge was plainly irritated by the pettiness of those who accused Patience. Twice she had swooned in the heat and the court stood in recess. He permitted the doors and windows to be opened over the witch finder's strenuous protests.

Any who could lay hands upon a sheet of paper were allowed to use it as a fan as the trial continued through the long, hot afternoon.

Finally it appeared that Judge Grimsted had had his fill of the proceedings. "I think this trial may be in error." The witch finder, on his left, began to protest but thought better of it. The judge continued: "Throughout these proceedings, Mistress Cory has carried herself well. She has cursed none and not blasphemed. She shrinks not at God's holy name.

"The learned men tell us a witch cannot weep, yet Mistress Cory can. Christ shed amorous tears upon the Cross, and his mother wept over his body. No witch therefore can weep; the Devil specifically forbids it.

"The prisoner was watched; a rat came into the cell, but it did not approach any of those present, rather it ran away at once.

"She was searched, but no witch marks were found. No teat was discovered from which her familiar spirit could draw its ration of blood."

A great stillness had descended on the room. "She was not pricked," said the witch finder, fearing the loss of his victim. "Let me insert pins in her, and I will find a spot insensitive to pain, a place that will not bleed."

"No!" Judge Grimsted's color was rising. "Much deception has been practiced by prickers. I have myself seen a bodkin which permits the blade to slide into the handle, thus giving the impression of entering the flesh when it does not in fact do so."

The door in the back of the meetinghouse burst open. In came Joshua McKay, striding confidently to the jury table carrying a small sack. Without ceremony he dropped it in front of Judge Grimsted. "You want proof; I'll give it to you." And so saying, he upended the bag. Out fell an assortment of items including an onion, a supply of pins and beads, a lock of hair, several candles, three dried ears of corn, and several pieces of brightly colored fabric.

"What be these trifles?" the judge asked, waving a hand at them.

Matthew Beverley was on his feet, eagerly sifting through the objects. "These, my lord, be the means whereby a witch shall be brought to justice."

Many of the people began pressing around the judge's table. "They look innocent enough," said the judge.

"They are items the Devil instructs his witches to use to make images of their enemies," said the witch finder, picking

193

up the onion. "The witch inscribes a name on a piece of paper and puts the onion behind the wall near the chimney or in the ovens of the fireplace. As it withers"—he held up the onion and slowly stripped off a dozen shreds—"so does the victim die."

The judge looked doubtful but said nothing. Seizing his opportunity, Beverley continued. "These ears of dried maize they dress with cloth and draw on them a face to resemble their enemy and call them poppets. A lock of hair from the object of their venom increases the power of the doll." Seeing he had gained their attention, he brandished one of the ears above his head and thundered. "Then they stick pins in the little dolls and victims are afflicted where the pin enters. They spit on them, for spittle is believed to have occult power."

The judge had come to his decision. "These are but sundries found in the house of anyone in this courtroom. I ask Master McKay why he brought these items before the court."

"And I ask," Jared shouted, "by what right he enters another's dwelling without permission."

There was a chorus of approval from around the room.

"And he sick and maybe dying," cried a voice from the back of the hall. "Shame."

"I sent him," admitted Beverley, when quiet was restored.

"And told him what to bring?" demanded the judge.

Beverley nodded. "Yet these be the instruments of great maliciousness and death. In Salem, the judges discovered two of these poppets and set fire to the dress of one, and the afflicted was burned on the leg. Another was held under water, and the afflicted strove for breath as if drowning."

"If that be the case," retorted Jared, "the power is not in the witch but in the doll. Why punish some foolish old woman who possesses no power of witching? And," he said, turning to the villagers, "if the judges were as successful as you claim, let them be prosecuted for witchcraft."

A fresh uproar burst forth. Arguments raged among neighbors, and blows were likely to have been struck had not the judge threatened to fine them all. Even so the clamor and confusion lasted some time. Some wished to tell what they knew of Patience, others had tales of witchcraft to relate. And there was considerable wailing of the very young children, who wished to be taken home, as they had attended long hours without knowing what their elders were about.

When the constable restored calm, the judge stood and sent for the Bible from the lectern and rested his hands atop the great leather binding. A solemn hush descended upon the room. "I cannot tell," he said, "whether the charges be true or false, though I believe the latter. There is, however, a test. We know witches recite the Lord's Prayer from St. Matthew's Gospel. They do, however, recite it *backward*. If Mistress Cory can recite the prayer twice in its correct form, without pause, I shall declare her innocent."

Jared protested. "She is exhausted; she has barely slept. . . ."

"Let me do it," Patience pleaded, rising unsteadily to her feet. In a tired but clear voice she began:

> "Our Father which art in heaven,
> Hallowed be thy name.
> Thy kingdom come.
> Thy will be done on earth as it is in
>   Heaven.
> Give us this day our daily bread.
> And forgive us our debtors . . . forgive . . ."

She broke off. Jared looked into her face in an agony of doubt.

> "And forgive us our debtors
> As we forgive our debts.

I mean, 'Forgive us our debts—' "

"She doesn't know it," crowed the witch finder triumphantly. "She has failed the test."

"Give her a moment," Jared pleaded with Judge Grimsted. "She's overwrought."

To Patience it seemed as if she were spinning round and round. The room revolved, a blur of faces, the judges' table, the walls, the doors. She was too weary, too confused, too disoriented. She stopped spinning and felt herself falling through the air. The light faded. She was plunging into a bottomless pit on wings of darkness. Gratefully she fainted away, leaving Jared clinging to her unconscious body.

She never heard the verdict: guilty.

"Wake up, Hannah." Her aunt was shaking her gently by the arm. "You should be in bed, child."

Hannah looked about her in amazement. She was in the Cadillac, her aunt looking down at her. "Didn't you see, didn't ..." Her voice trailed off. "I guess it was another dream."

"What was, child?"

"Oh, nothing," Hannah replied. "I guess I ought to be going to bed. Thank you for a lovely evening."

Five minutes later she was fast asleep. And there were no more dreams.

16
Decision

HANNAH SAT OPPOSITE DR. MARSH. THE DOCTOR had agreed to see her the minute she had called from West Tisbury and had not moved while Hannah told her of her dreams. She had not touched any of the neatly stacked packs of sugarless gum on the little table in front of her. When Hannah finished, there was a long pause. Dr. Marsh gestured with her hands as if trying to grasp something with them. "Everything you have told me fits exactly with what I gathered when I first hypnotized you."

Hannah sat bolt upright. "Everything?"

"As far as I can tell. Many of the things you've told me seem to fit a pattern, especially the dreams. But there is much beyond my clinical experience." She leaned forward, as if imparting a secret. "There was a girl called Mary Thompsett, or was it Louise? I could never tell them apart. One day she fell at the skating rink and hit her head on the ice. It was forty-eight hours before she recovered consciousness. When she did, Mary was talking in Welsh. That wasn't the most interesting part. When she was asked her name she said 'Blodwin Jones' and said the year was 1820."

Hannah sat very still taking it all in. "What happened?" she asked, in a small voice.

"She recovered and forgot all her Welsh. Blows to the head have unpredictable results. The odd thing was, of course, she was remembering something that could not possibly have happened to her."

Hannah was puzzled. "Then how could she remember it?"

Dr. Marsh tapped agitatedly on the arm of her chair with her fingers. "No one knows. There are all sorts of half-baked theories. And when I regressed you in an attempt to discover what was causing your dreams, you acted like Mary. You became someone else, and you seem to be having memories of her life and time. This Puritan girl, called Patience, has projected her life into yours. It appears you can help her in some way."

"Is this reincarnation? I've heard of that."

Dr. Marsh didn't answer; absently she picked up a packet of gum, twisting it slowly in her hands before carefully placing it on the table in front of her. "Lots of important people believe in reincarnation, but I do not. I believe there is something going on here that needs investigating for your sake. I don't think you'll have any peace of mind until you know why you are dreaming these things."

There was a long silence. Finally the doctor said, "Your dreams tell the same story as you do to me under hypnosis. You can remember the dreams, and things are happening to you that support the idea that you are experiencing what witches suffered in the past. The burning pain in your shoulder suggests the branding of a witch. You have constrictions in your throat; this hysterical reaction was thought to be brought on by the Devil pouring poisons down his victim's throat."

Hannah shuddered in spite of herself. "But I didn't know anything about those things."

Dr. Marsh leaned forward in her chair. "That's what is so puzzling," she said earnestly. "It's as if you didn't dream the events, but lived them. And the problems began after you came to the Vineyard."

She looked into the distance, clearly thinking deeply. "Hannah, you could have learned about these things and by some trick of memory recalled them under hypnosis. One thing these cases have in common is the patients' claim to be people so ordinary no one can check on them. You might, for instance, have remembered Patience's history from a book."

"But I haven't," Hannah protested. "I've never heard of Patience Cory."

"I know, I know." Dr. Marsh held the girl's hands between her own. "It's your decision, but I think you know what you must do."

Hannah searched her face. "You mean let myself be hypnotized again."

"Only if you want to."

"On one condition," Hannah replied.

"And that is?"

"We do it here and now."

17
A Promise

FOUR.

Three.

Two.

One.

They came for Patience a week after the verdict. She visited her father despite the objections of Matthew Beverley.

Nothing had prepared her for the shattered old man lying in his bed not knowing her, perhaps even unaware of her presence. Eyes once clear and steady were now blank. His once clear, commanding voice muttered incoherently some message that none, least of all he, would understand.

Silently she allowed herself to be led back to her cell.

The sun had been up some half an hour, and its rays were shining through the chinks in the wall, when Patience heard the bolts withdrawn and the door opened.

The night before, she had spoken to Jared; Judge Grimsted had specifically ordered it before he left for the mainland. Some said he was going because he could not bear to see an innocent person hanged.

She could not stop weeping. "What's happening?" Patience asked through her tears. "Why can't I stop crying?"

"It's grief," he told her, holding her tightly to him. "You may grieve; it will cleanse you." And Patience wept in his arms.

When, finally, the tears stopped, she spoke. "Jared, what will you do?"

In his despair, he shook his head.

Their lips met for the first time. When they parted, Patience said, "I want you to live. You have a choice. You must forget me. You must live."

They sat in the straw. Patience said, "Oh, Jared, if only I could prove my innocence. Nothing matters to me so much as that my friends and neighbors should know I am no wicked person."

"Who doubts your innocence?" protested Jared. "Only a few sour, ignorant malcontents."

"I just wish I could . . . I feel I shall never rest until I have proved my innocence to one honest person."

On the evening before sentence was to be carried out, they met for the last time. Jared spoke of love. Then he talked of hope. He had laid a charge of unchastity against Judith McKay and sworn out a warrant before Minister Slaughter accusing Judith of sundry acts of lewd behavior. Now he admitted it was his discovery of these deeds that had led to the breach between them. "It is all my fault, Patience," he whispered. "It is to spite me. Judith accuses you to get at me."

It was dark in the cell; only one guttering candle was permitted. Patience could just see Jared's face in the gloom. She touched his hand.

"Jared, please don't attack Judith. It will not help me, and I will not go lightly to the scaffold knowing another person's reputation is to be ruined."

"There is a way," urged Jared. "You must confess. Tell them you are in league with Satan. Offer to repent, and the sentence will be reduced."

Patience gave his hand a gentle squeeze. "But it would be a lie, Jared. All that I have is my honor; I will not abandon that now. It is our way. If we lose our honor, what have we? Most, if not all, of those accused of witching could confess falsely and save their lives. Yet they do not. What is a life worth without self-respect?"

At this, Jared knew she would never be his, but he made one final effort. "But Patience, what of our love? If you die, what is to become of me?"

Patience's head was on his chest; Jared's arms encircled her body, his strength protecting her. Fighting back her tears, she answered. "You must make a new life." She looked up into his face, her lashes wet and golden. "You must. I have learned to accept suffering. We do not know God's purpose, but we must accept His will.

"Now I want you to go away. If you love me, please do not come tomorrow, for my courage will fail me if you do. Say no more, but go." Taking his hand, she kissed it tenderly, then turned away knowing she would not see him again on earth. Jared would have held her, but realizing it would destroy her, he left quickly.

Then the storm broke within her, a flood of tears rolled

down her cheeks, and she tasted the salt. And in the corner of her cell she spent the rest of the night in prayer.

Matthew Beverley had not stayed to celebrate his triumph. News was he was in Salem Village on the mainland, where more children were afflicted. Reverend Slaughter, his face drawn and pale, had come to the cell with three of the village elders to see if she would confess at the last. When she asked about her father, they spared her the truth, speaking optimistically of a full recovery. Then out of the hearing of his companions, the minister murmured, "Mistress Cory, you may claim to be with child. They cannot hang the innocent babe. 'Tis often done. Then, when tempers cool, you—"

"I would rather be hanged as a witch than gain the reputation of a harlot," she answered sharply. "Surely you, above all, know how important the truth is. Does not the Good Book say 'the truth shall set you free'?" The minister coughed and said no more. The men retired from the cell.

"Make yourself ready, Patience," said the jailer's wife. "I've brought you fresh water and a comb." She began to untangle Patience's knotted hair, combing it as best she could. Patience ignored the pain of the almost constant tugging. Nothing could bring back its luster, but now at least it hung loose and free.

A towel and water cleansed her face. And all the while, Patience tried not to show the fear that gnawed away inside her.

They took her to Witch Hill, a mile from the village. A patient donkey pulled her cart steadily along the common and took the path through the Great West Field to Witch Hill, most villagers walking silently behind.

When the cart's wheels stuck in a rut, there was a painful

silence, for it might have been an attempt by Satan to protect his creature. No one wanted to say this, and many felt ashamed of thinking it. But the cart was soon free and finally it stood beneath the great oak on top of the hill.

She embraced many friends old and new, afraid to become too emotional, for the tears were barely held back. Jared, true to his love and promise, was not there. For this, she would be forever grateful. "Thank you, Jared," she murmured. "Farewell, my love."

The jailer helped her back into the cart. "I didn't mean to be so harsh, Patience," he said to her. "It's just that when we lost little Prudence I thought of witching. I know you're no witch."

"Thank you," she answered. "I do not blame you."

For the last time, Patience stood facing her accusers. The minister read the verdict. She heard a few phrases: "familiarity with Satan," "doing harm by magic," "tormenting by poppets"; but none of it mattered now.

Minister Slaughter had a black bandage to cover her eyes. She refused it, stepping to the front of the cart.

"I forgive those who accused me and my judges. I am innocent, and I would give all I have to prove it. Never in my life did I tell a lie." There was much uneasiness in the crowd, for this they knew to be true.

"It is said that I and the others in the jail are in league with the Devil. There may be witches, I know not. The Lord direct you in pursuit of them if it be his will. I pray you will investigate most closely, for many confess to what cannot be so. I do not confess, for I have ever told the truth."

Now several women were sobbing and many men looked shamefaced at the ground, kicking at the soil with their boots.

Then she recited the Lord's Prayer without a tremor.

The jailer gently knotted a rope around her wrists and directed her to stand in the center of the cart.

"It will soon be time," Minister Slaughter said to her, as the hangman tied a cord around her ankles. "Will you not confess?"

"I cannot confess to a crime I have not committed," she replied.

The minister sighed. "If you only had proof." Opening his Bible, he began to read from the Book of Revelation. The jailer slipped the rope around her neck, arranging her hair over it.

The crowd was now silent; no one moved, here at the last. The jailer jumped down from the cart and raised his hand to give the donkey a sharp slap on its hindquarters.

The minister's voice rose in anticipation of the sudden lurching forward of donkey and cart, the sudden stretching of the rope, the . . .

"And I heard a great voice out of heaven saying, 'Behold, the tabernacle of God is with men, and He will dwell with them . . .'" He turned the page. The movement caught Patience's eye. Then she knew what it was she wanted to tell them. In that instant she knew she could prove her innocence. Jared could still be hers. "Bible," she cried out. "I remember! My Bible. I must have my Bible. I can . . ."

The minister pressed his Bible into her hands.

"No! No! My own Bible, it has—"

And those were the last words she spoke.

18
A Witch
Across Time

July 20,
1692

July 20,
1990

From a long way off, a voice was calling to her. The words were muffled, as if the speaker were holding a pillow over his mouth. Hannah heard her name; she wanted to answer but could not frame the words.

"Four."

"Three."

Now the words were clear and close.

"Two."

"One."

There was the sound of fingers snapping in her ear. Then her eyes opened. Dr. Marsh was looking very intently at her. "Are you all right, Hannah?"

"I'm fine," she replied. "Did you hear everything?"

"Hear anything? You had just gone into trance, and then you started shouting for a Bible. I brought you out immediately."

"But," said Hannah in amazement, "I must have been gone for hours. And this time I can remember every detail."

"Less than ten seconds."

Hannah told Dr. Marsh everything she could recall; the psychiatrist shook her head in disbelief. "It's as if a whole life flashed before your eyes in seconds."

"Do you think it was a regression?"

The doctor pursed her lips. "I believe it's something different. At some point in your life you learned Patience's story, and it affected you profoundly. You wanted to keep Patience alive, so you let her live in you. The hypnosis drew out the story of Patience because that was the story we were both interested in."

Hannah got out of the chair and walked to the window. "It was so real. I was someone else." Shaking her head, she looked at the bonsai trees. "It was so real."

"It's the most incredible story I've ever heard, Hannah, but it doesn't explain why you have visions of Patience at Stewart's Grove. Of course, timbers from her father's house were used to build the bakehouse, that's clear enough."

Hannah turned back to the doctor. "Patience wanted to tell me something. She must have waited in the old part of the house until she found someone sympathetic enough to listen. After all, I couldn't possibly have known all those details of the trial."

"You could have imagined it all," suggested the doctor, doubt in her voice. "There's no way to prove what happened without some independent record to substantiate what you saw."

"She must have," Hannah insisted. "Patience is trying to tell me something, and I mean to find out what."

Dr. Marsh marveled at the change in Hannah. What had happened to the insecure creature of a few days ago? She stood. "Let's call it a day. On Wednesday, at eleven, we'll go on from here and see if we can make more sense of it."

Mrs. Donohue was waiting at the high-school parking lot.

"Greg's back," she said without any preamble, taking an envelope from her purse. "His cousin, Amy, suddenly decided to get married." She shook her head. "Just like that. Typical! So he went to Oak Bluffs yesterday for the wedding. He brought back some of those instant photograph things."

Her hands trembling, Hannah sorted through the Polaroids. There was Greg grinning slightly self-consciously in suit and tie, next to the bride and groom. Looking very beautiful and very interested in her new husband was the girl Hannah had seen Greg with at the ice-cream parlor!

"Don't think much of those immediate cameras. We didn't have them . . ."

"Before the war," Hannah finished, planting a kiss on the cheek of the astonished Mrs. Donohue.

"Good Lord, child, what's got into you?" The housekeeper started the Buick. "I'll never understand modern kids."

Hannah sorted through the pictures feeling supremely happy.

"Big do, that," said Mrs. Donohue, turning on to the main road. "Lots of money, the Mallorys. Pity none of it came into our family." A bicycle wobbled in front of her; she passed the rider, missing him by inches. "I certainly didn't marry any money, that's for sure."

"Your husband was in the army, wasn't he?"

"The army?"

"During the war; he was injured."

The horn blared out, a pair of backpackers moved swiftly out of their way. Mrs. Donohue shot Hannah a puzzled look. "Never. He wasn't in the army. He had flat feet. They made him a mechanic. Just as well, too. Mrs. Chase has told him to fix that crazy fountain. Why would he say he was in the army? Beats me."

Hannah sat back happily. She knew why and she was grateful. Best of all, Greg would soon be back. She was brought back to the real world by a familiar grinding gearshift.

"Why is the fountain being turned on?"

"Oh la-di-da! Someone she met is coming to dinner. A widower. We must be at our best. Can't imagine why."

Hannah smiled all the way to Stewart's Grove, much to Mrs. Donohue's mystification.

She found Greg painting shutters. "I can't kiss you," he said playfully. "I've got paint on my hands."

Hannah kissed him anyway, and Greg made a big thing of holding his hands above his head. "I was at a wedding," he said. "It was very sudden or I would have asked you to go."

"I heard," Hannah said. "And Mrs. Donohue showed me some pictures."

They sat on one of the unpainted shutters, and Hannah told him the story of Patience. Greg shook his head doubtfully. "Do you believe in regression? It doesn't make any sense."

"No, it doesn't because we don't want it to. Somehow the story of Patience Cory has become part of my life, and I have no memory of ever hearing about her."

Greg wiped his hand on a rag. "I want to believe it, but what you're saying is impossible. Yet there's got to be some other explanation."

Hannah shook her head decisively. "Who cares what the explanation is? Patience needs my help. She's made this tremendous effort to contact me. What I was seeing was *her* life, not some vision of my own."

"So what's the plan?" He stuck his brush in a jar of turpentine. "I suppose these shutters can wait."

"Oh, hang your shutters," Hannah said passionately. "Patience lived and worked in the old part of the house. She led me to the bakehouse. There must be something there. I'm going to see what I can find."

"I'm coming with you," Greg said. "I'll get a flashlight. We won't be seen if we go by Long Walk. But there isn't anything in that room except an old table and an antique fireplace."

"There must be something. That's why Patience led me there."

Greg dug in his toolbox and took out a flashlight and a hammer. "Just in case we meet Caspar the unfriendly ghost," he said, with a grin.

They made their way down Long Walk. There were traces of their last journey in the dust, and the statues were as inscrutable as ever. "I don't suppose this part of the house will ever be open again," said Greg. "It's kinda sad, really."

"I never thought the fountain would be turned on," said Hannah, "but it is. No reason things can't change at Stewart's Grove," she added confidently.

"You're right," Greg agreed. Did she imagine a note of respect in his voice? "This way."

They found the bakehouse without difficulty; it was as barren as ever. Some light filtered in from the dirty skylight.

"Try tapping the walls," she suggested. "There may be a space behind."

He moved all around the room, tapping with the hammer, but no sign of a secret panel or hollow spot was found. The floor came next. They pursued their search, breaking the silence only with taps of the hammer. The floor was solid stone.

"Well?" asked Greg, sitting on the table. "What now, fearless leader?"

Hannah looked around the room. There was only one place left. "Fireplace," she said with determination.

Greg slid off the table and surveyed the fireplace. It was a great iron construction with elaborate grillwork.

"Looks pretty solid to me," he said.

Hannah was inspecting it closely. "Look," she said, aiming the light. Greg examined the spot carefully. "David Lake Forge, 1820," he read. "So this isn't the original."

Using the hammer, Greg pried away the edges. There was a loud grinding sound as the ironwork came loose. Behind was the wooden frame of a much older fireplace. Half an hour's prying and levering clearly revealed the outline of the original fireplace. The nineteenth-century iron fireplace had been fitted over it and much of the original bricked up.

Hannah was reaching behind the elaborate grillwork. "I can't . . ."

"Wait," Greg said. "Let's not be too fussy. Stand back."

Hannah retreated to the far side of the room; Greg took hold of the edge of the ironwork and pulled. There was a loud rending sound. The metal came away from the wall behind it. "Here we go," he said, giving another wrench.

The entire iron fireplace swayed and then fell forward with an earsplitting crash. Pieces of wrought-iron carving snapped like twigs.

"Oh boy," Greg said, jumping backward in alarm. "My God. Just look at this mess, will you? If Mrs. Chase ever comes down here . . ."

Hannah was too intent on her quest to respond. She sensed, though, that Greg found it hard to believe that the determined young woman beside him was the same Hannah Kincaid he'd first met less than two weeks ago.

Stepping over the scattered pieces of broken ironwork, Hannah felt along the top of the original mantelpiece. It was very deep, about two feet, and the far edge did not touch the wall. It had pulled away, leaving a gap some two inches wide. When this had happened there was no way of knowing, but as Hannah felt along the gap, her fingers touched something.

Very carefully, she tightened her fingers around the object, already knowing what it was.

"The Bible," said Greg in astonishment. "You knew all the time."

"I think I did," said Hannah, almost overcome with excitement. "Patience must have put it on the mantelpiece, and it slipped down the gap behind."

Greg opened it. "Matthew, chapter 12, verse seven. 'But if ye had known what *this* meaneth, I will have mercy, and not sacrifice, ye would not have condemned the guiltless.' Strong stuff."

Hannah took the book from him. "But why is it so important?"

"You don't know?"

Hannah shook her head. "Patience wasn't looking for just

any Bible; she wanted *hers*. There must be something here to clear her name. She can't rest until her innocence is proved." Turning to the end pages, she saw faded writing in a small, neat script.

"There's something written inside the cover," she said. "A family history by the look of it. The ink has faded."

Greg looked over her shoulder. There were a half dozen names and dates. Then Hannah saw it. Written at the top of the page was "Martinmas, 1691, Ezra Proctor born, attn birth, Boston, P.C."

She didn't see it at once, but the date nagged at her. Martinmas. She had heard of that day before. "Martinmas," she said, loudly. "Martinmas."

"What about it?"

"It's obvious," she said, hugging him in her excitement. "Judith accused Patience of bewitching her the day before Martinmas. But Patience was in Boston a day later. She couldn't have made the journey in a day. The Bible is the proof that Judith was lying."

Greg let out a low whistle. "So Patience *was* framed."

"And now we know what she meant."

"Well, it won't help Patience much," Greg pointed out.

Hannah snuggled up close to him. "Oh yes it will. She wanted *me* to know she was innocent. That will be enough. Wherever she is, she won't have to worry about the past. And death isn't the end of things after all. It's a promise. Patience is telling us we don't disappear, we live again."

Hannah didn't know it, but her cheeks were wet with tears. She was grieving for her mother, saying good-bye to childhood.

She knew now that she had expected too much of herself

and others. She'd seen Greg as the ideal boyfriend, she'd seen her father as the perfect father, and she had tried to be the perfect daughter, taking her mother's place after her death.

When her father had remarried, Hannah had felt overwhelmed because he didn't mourn her mother forever. When she'd thought Greg had thrown her over for someone else, it had devastated her. She expected life to be fair, but it wasn't. Patience's cruel fate showed that.

Hannah knew it was she who had to change, not others. She had to accept people for what they were—not what she would like them to be. And she *could* accept it.

Greg stood silently by, his arms encircling her. In that moment they understood each other completely. Greg held her for a long time before gently pressing his lips to hers; she responded eagerly. And when they left hand in hand, she closed the bakehouse door behind them.

Perhaps no one would ever venture into this part of the house again. It would collect dust, it would fall into complete disrepair, finally it would be no more than a memory.

Yet, for an instant, two lives had merged across a gulf of time.

Now Patience was at peace, and Hannah too.

Epilogue

Dear H,

Guess what? I'M CURED!!!!

I got the word yesterday. I'm outta here. Weekly shrink visits, of course. It's a bit scary, isn't it? My dad's coming up to get me. I talked to him on the phone, and he says you can stay with us all summer if you like. I know you won't, of course, because you've got a man!! WHERE'S THE PICTURE OF THE HUNK? Will you spend a week with a healthy old friend?

Oh God it's so good to be going home. Chris has already said he'll visit me.

Mrs. Pascoe has resumed inventory of the books. I'm getting out of here just in time. Your name came up because you had a very

215

old book called *Little Known Witches of New England.* A rare first edition, very limited publication. I put in a phony card for you.

LATER!

Lots of love,

M.

P.S. SAVED! The book you lost was found in the reading room. The old fireplace was being demolished, and it had slipped behind the grate. Weird! But truth is stranger than fiction. And, best of all, life goes on.